LUCK *of the* POLISH

LUCK *of the* POLISH

Irene Pitura

Order this book online at www.trafford.com
or email orders@trafford.com

Most Trafford titles are also available at major online book retailers.

Printed in the United States of America.

ISBN: 978-1-4669-0729-4 (sc)
ISBN: 978-1-4669-0730-0 (hc)
ISBN: 978-1-4669-0731-7 (e)

Library of Congress Control Number: 2011962183

Trafford rev. 12/21/2011

 www.trafford.com

North America & international
toll-free: 1 888 232 4444 (USA & Canada)
phone: 250 383 6864 ♦ fax: 812 355 4082

CHAPTER 1

MARISHA GLANCED AT the bedside clock—2.15 a.m. "Dammit! Why can't I sleep?" Dragging herself out of bed, she went to the kitchen and plugged in the electric kettle. "Maybe some herbal tea will relax me," she thought. It hadn't done the trick last night, or the night before, but it seemed worth trying again. "Maybe it will work tonight." She was hopeful.

Lately, sleeping had been a problem. Every night, she'd go to bed and fall asleep immediately. An hour or two later she'd wake up and remain sleepless until the morning. Lack of proper rest at night had made her tired and irritable during the day.

"I should get a night job," she thought with a sigh. "No, I just have too much on my mind, that's all. Aunt Sonia would say that I can't sleep because I have a guilty conscience. Aunt Sonia . . . God! What made me think of her?"

Thinking about Aunt Sonia gave Marisha an idea. She decided to find the diary she had started when she was a teenager and was still living in Poland. "If reading it doesn't put me to sleep, at least I'll have something to do until the morning comes," she thought.

The whistle from the kettle made her jump. Pouring hot water over the tea bag, she tried to remember the last place she'd seen her diary. She knew she still had it, but where was it?

Returning to the bedroom and setting the teacup on the bedside table, Marisha walked over to the closet. "It has to be in here," she concluded, opening the closet door.

On the top shelf, next to her neatly folded sweaters, there were six small storage boxes. Reading the labels, she located the one she was looking for. *Aha!* Pulling the bottom box labelled "Poland," she set it on the floor and lifted the lid. "It must be ten years since I have seen this stuff," she thought.

The first thing in the box was a beautiful embroidered tablecloth her Aunt Sonia had made especially for her. Marisha picked up the material and studied it with appreciative eyes. "Many hours were spent making this," she recalled.

Remembering how surprised she had been when she'd received the gift, Marisha's eyes filled with tears. She buried her face in the fabric and forced her memory to bring forth Aunt Sonia's image. Dark and unrecognizable at first, slowly, her relative's frowning face came into focus. Shivers ran up and down Marisha's spine. She opened her eyes. Why would seeing her aunt's face make her this uncomfortable? Guilt? Regrets? Perhaps . . . hate?

Placing the tablecloth gently on the carpet, she looked into the box again. "Wow, this is all that's left from my life in Poland."

Choking back tears, she reached in and one by one, lifted the items out of the box, pausing for a brief moment to recall why she'd kept those things, what made each item special enough to be kept. There wasn't much to look back on; a novel, her old passport, a hair clip, two ribbons, a Moda fashion magazine, plane tickets, a black and white picture of her parents, and a small sum of Polish money. The diary completed her collection of memorabilia.

Marisha picked up the picture of her parents and gently touched their faces with the tips of her fingers. "How would my life have turned out if they didn't die? I'd be living in Poland; maybe I'd be married, have children . . . or would I?"

As it was, at forty-three, she was still single. She'd gone to the altar three times, but each time she had left the church single. A few months ago, after yet another failed attempt at marriage, she'd convinced herself that she was cursed. She believed a black cloud of punishment hung over her head, preventing any chance of happiness. It had to be Aunt Martha's curse, or maybe Aunt Sonia's. Whatever the reason, Marisha had given up finding a husband and had decided to concentrate on her career. After all, what was the point in wishing for something that simply wasn't meant to be? Even if by some stroke of luck she'd found a man who'd marry her, what good would it do? Could she give him children? Surely, her biological clock was well past that hour! She couldn't defeat her fate.

Shaking the dreary thoughts from her mind, Marisha replaced her memorabilia in the box. After a short struggle to put the box back on the top shelf, she pushed the closet doors shut. Stepping back, she caught her reflection in the mirrored door panels. Who was this woman looking back at her? What was her reason for being? As if the answers to her questions were written deeply inside her eyes, she stared intently into their blue pools. Someone claimed that eyes were the windows to one's soul. All she saw in her eyes was emptiness and sorrow. Yet, a few men had told her that she had beautiful eyes and that she was beautiful and sexy. Taking her gaze away from her face, Marisha turned her body sideways and studied her figure. Five foot six inches tall and slimly built, but what would make anyone think that she was beautiful and sexy? Bouncing her shoulder-length blonde hair and pursing her full lips, Marisha scanned her image from head to toe. In her opinion, her figure was average. Her legs were shapely and stomach flat, but her breasts were an average size, 34B. "Isn't sexy another word for big breasted?" Turning her back to the mirror, she checked her backside. "Well, I guess it's not too bad. Nothing's heading south yet." She pulled a face at her reflection and left the room in search of her reading glasses.

Returning to the bedroom, she climbed into bed and picked up the old notebook. Running her fingers over the worn cover, she thought, "Where did the time go? Poland was just yesterday and yet a million years ago." Eyes closed, she rested her head against the pillows. "Was it a good idea to go back in time?" How would she feel reliving the past through her own words? For a moment, she considered putting the book back into the box. Then she made up her mind. "For heaven's sake, this is ridiculous! Why should I worry about reading my own diary? It was my life, I wrote about it! Heck, I lived it!" Marisha flipped over the cover page with determination. Inside, written in huge letters was her name, age and birthday, September 20th 1959. Her hand shook a little when she picked up the teacup. Taking a sip of the amber liquid, she read the first entry.

Sept. 20th, 1974

Dear Diary,

Today is my fifteenth birthday. I'm sad to say that nobody knows about it. It's not a big deal though. No one ever remembers my birthdays anyway. Well, only once, when I was nine, my dad had remembered, and he gave me a present—a doll. That was the last time.

Yesterday, I found this notebook in the attic, and to my surprise, nothing is written in it—all the pages are empty. I've decided that today, on my birthday, I'll start writing a diary.

My life is not very exciting, but since I don't have anyone to talk to, this diary will be my friend and confidante. Besides, writing every day will give me something to look forward to. Well, diary, here we go.

Let's start with me telling you about the first fifteen years of my life—what I can remember of them, anyway.

I was born in Tarnica on September 20th 1959. Tarnica is a small village in Poland, where my parents, Jan and Sophie Pawlak, owned a little farm.

I don't remember the first few years of my life. All I can tell you is that my dad worked in the fields most of the time, my mom stayed at home with me, and that I was their only child.

Sometimes, mom and I would go to the fields to help dad. I remember watching my parents hoe potatoes, or pull out white sugar beets from the ground and with huge knives, cut off the beet tops. I was too little to help with that kind of work, but after the potatoes or the beets were dug up and scattered all over the field, I would help mom put them into big baskets. Then we'd throw them onto a wooden wagon. We didn't have a tractor back then, so my dad used horses to pull the wagon.

My mom died when I was five years old. To this day, I have no idea why. She wasn't sick or anything. Dad said that he'd explain her death to me when I got older, but he died shortly after my ninth birthday and I guess now I'll never know. At least I know how he died.

After mom's funeral, dad started to drink a lot of vodka. He didn't look after the animals or the farm any more, and things started to go bad. One of our horses broke his leg and had to be shot. Somebody's dog got into the chicken coup and killed most of our chickens. Our house was always a mess and everything was falling apart. Some people tried to help us, but dad wouldn't let them. "We don't take charity," he'd say.

I know he was missing mom, and since I resemble her, it was hard for him to be around me. I have no doubt that he loved me, but towards the end, he couldn't even look at me. He'd go to the village a lot and I was left at home by myself. When I asked him why he didn't stay at home or work in the fields like he did before, he told me that there was nothing to work for any more and since I looked so much like mom it made him sad when he was with me.

When I was seven, my dad's younger sister, Rose, came to live with us. I started school that year and my Aunt Rose looked after the house. My dad was still drinking a lot, but he had started to take better care of the farm. For a while, I thought that things would get back to normal.

As I've told you before, on my ninth birthday, dad gave me a present. I had never gotten a birthday present before, or at least I don't remember getting one, so I was very excited. My present was a doll. She was soft, had curly blonde hair and beautiful blue eyes that opened and closed. I'd never had a doll like her before. I named her India. I know it's a strange name for a doll and I have no idea why I chose it but at that time, I thought it was perfect for her.

That birthday was very special for me; my dad even hugged and kissed me. He hadn't done that in a long time.

Two months after my birthday, Aunt Rose, just like my mom, didn't wake up from her sleep. Two days after that, my dad went to the barn and shot himself.

The day of dad's and Aunt Rose's funerals, I was surprised to learn that they came from a big family. Dad had four brothers and six sisters. Aunt Rose was dead and Aunt Martha and Uncle Joseph were living in Canada, but the rest of them came to the funeral with their wives, husbands and their children, except for Aunt Sonia. She didn't have a husband or kids. She came alone.

It was nice to meet my cousins. Too bad it had to be at my dad's funeral. I wished I had met them under happier circumstances.

The night of the funerals, after the kids were sent to bed, my aunts and uncles gathered in our living room for a family meeting. From my bedroom, I heard them arguing about something. They were arguing for many hours. I couldn't make out what they were arguing about, but I remember how scared I was. They sounded as though they hated each other.

Marisha set the diary on her lap. Closing her eyes, she could almost hear the steady hum of her relatives' voices. She remembered how scared she had felt that night—scared and alone. Sharing a bedroom with four other girls was somewhat comforting but it didn't make her feel safe. All the people in her house were relatives but they were strangers, and she felt very alone.

She searched her memory for the images of the cousins sharing her room that night. Two of the girls were Uncle Peter's and Aunt

Bettie's children. The other two were Uncle Zen's. Her cousins had parents, brothers and sisters and she remembered how envious she had been of them that night.

Checking the alarm clock, Marisha noticed her forgotten tea. Taking a sip, she set it back on the table. The tea was too cold to enjoy.

It was 3.49 a.m. Not yet tired, she picked up the diary and continued reading.

In the middle of the night, I woke up to the sound of crying. It was my cousin Anna. She was having a bad dream or something. Her mother came in and woke her up. She put Anna on her lap and rocked her gently in her arms. I remembered my mom holding me like that. I felt so warm and secure in her arms. God, I miss her so much! Why did she have to die and leave me all alone?

I don't remember much of the next few days but somehow I ended up going to live with Aunt Sonia in a town called Lipa.

I was scared of my aunt. She was very tall and wrinkled and I could see her bones under the thin layer of her see-through skin. Her eyes were very strange too, like her hair—they were almost white. She looked mean and angry. Even her voice sounded scary when she talked.

That first day, as we walked to the train station, she warned me that she was fifty-eight years old, had never been married, and didn't know the first thing about children. However, she was positive that I would be a lot of work and expensive to keep. She also told me that she could barely afford to feed me, and I shouldn't expect any toys, clothes, or pocket money from her. Since I was almost ten years old,

I should earn my own money, help her around the house and stay out of trouble. After that speech, our four-hour train ride was completed in silence.

Aunt Sonia lives in a one-room apartment located on the second floor of an old, three-storey building. The building is nothing more than a bunch of red bricks barely held together by what is left of some cement mixture. Most of the concrete stairs leading to the second floor are cracked, chipped or missing altogether. The iron railings are rusted and bent, the plaster is falling from the walls, and the hallways are dark and scary. The apartment itself is not much better. The walls are damp, the ceiling is cracked, and the old wooden planks of the floor squeak when we step on them. By the window (which doesn't open), there is a crack big enough to fit my hand in. I would never put my hand in there though, because there are creatures living in it. I saw and heard them moving around. The worst part of it all is the bed, if you could call it a bed. I have to sleep with my aunt on a foldout sofa. Oh God, that is a nightmare! With springs digging into my ribs, and the sound of scraping rusted metal threatening to collapse any minute (not to mention Aunt Sonia's loud snoring), it's impossible for me to get much sleep. When I complain, I'm told that I'm spoiled and ungrateful and if I had a clear conscience, I would sleep peacefully.

I didn't like my aunt. I hated her apartment. Most of all, I hated my new school. The teachers were nasty and the kids were mean to me. One girl told me that they didn't like orphans. I didn't know what an orphan was and tried to tell her that I wasn't one, but she didn't believe me. She even called me a liar. I felt so stupid after Aunt Sonia explained that having no parents made me an orphan.

Embarrassed, I didn't want to go to school the next day or any day after that.

My aunt constantly complained about being old and sick. She never specified what was wrong with her, but she made me believe that she could drop dead at any moment. At first, I believed her. I tried my best to do everything for her. I cleaned, took out the garbage, went to the grocery store, whatever I could do to be helpful. She showed me how to do the laundry and how to cook, so I did that too. It was hard for me to bring the water in. The tap was downstairs, on the outside wall of the building, and carrying a full bucket up the broken stairs took every ounce of strength my ten-year-old body possessed. But no matter what I did, she was never happy. If that wasn't bad enough, she hired me out to her neighbours. I was a babysitter, cleaner, dog walker and cook. At the same time, I was going to school and helping her. The money I earned Aunt Sonia collected and kept for my upkeep. I didn't mind. Her constant complaining about feeding me made me feel very guilty. I didn't want to be a burden to her.

That first year, when school was out for the summer, Aunt Bettie came and took me to spend the summer at her house. I was happy to go with her. I thought I would get a break from all the cooking, cleaning and babysitting, and Aunt Sonia would have a break from me. I didn't know at that time that my summer vacation was just another business arrangement—that Aunt Bettie was renting me from Aunt Sonia. I was hired to look after my three little cousins and to help around the house.

For the past five years, every summer, I've gone from one relative to another. My job is always the same: cooking, cleaning, and looking after the children. Aunt Sonia told me that this was the only way she could afford to keep me. Now, I'm staying with Uncle Lech and Auntie Helen. They live on a farm. They have four children, three boys, aged two, four and six, and a five-month-old girl, Basia. I saw their oldest boy, Mark, when he was just a baby, at my dad's funeral.

It's nice to be on the farm again. It's so peaceful here, well, when the kids are napping, anyway. I came here this summer right after school was out, but I didn't go back to Lipa at the end of August. Aunt Helen is helping Uncle Lech with the harvest, and she really needs help with the children. Aunt Sonia sent me a letter to let me know that I didn't need to go back to school this year. She also said that she was very sick and couldn't look after me. She thought it would be best if I stayed here for a while longer. I don't understand why she thinks I'm so much work. If anything, I help her, but I'm happy that I don't have to go back to that school, and I don't mind being here.

I have my own room, well, sort of. It's just the attic of this old farmhouse, but I have privacy. I found some old furniture, books, and even some old clothes. I cleaned out one corner of the attic, made walls out of cardboard and old curtains, hung some old pictures, arranged the furniture, and dragged in an old mattress for a bed. The best thing about it is that I don't have to sleep with anyone, and the kids can't come in here. Even six-year-old Mark can't reach the ladder to the attic.

Well, that's enough for one day. I have to go to sleep now. Five o'clock comes fast, and I have to be up with the baby. The boys will sleep until seven-thirty, but the baby will be up when her parents wake up.

Marisha closed the book. Her eyelids were getting heavy now. "I should get a couple of hours of sleep or I'll be useless in the morning," she told herself.

The alarm clock was set for seven. It was five o'clock now.

CHAPTER 2

"YOU LOOK LIKE crap."

"Thanks . . . and good morning to you, too."

"No, really, I mean it. You look terrible. When are you going to talk to me?"

Lilly, an attractive, tall and slender blonde was getting annoyed with Marisha's refusal to confide in her. She had watched her friend sink deeper and deeper into depression, and not knowing what was wrong, she couldn't do anything to help.

"I've told you, when I'm ready, I'll talk to you." Marisha snapped at her.

"Marisha, you're my best friend. Please tell me what the heck is going on with you. You know me, I'm a good listener, and who knows, maybe I can help?"

"I'm your only friend."

"Ouch!"

"Sorry. I didn't mean it to sound like that. No, you can't help. Look, I have to go. I'll see you at lunch—are we still on?" Marisha asked timidly.

"Yeah, sure, see you at noon." Lilly picked up two small pieces of paper, bowed humbly, and handed them to Marisha.

"Your messages . . . ma'am."

"Cute, very cute" Marisha made a face at her friend, snatched the messages, and pointing her nose towards the ceiling, walked away.

Lilly watched her friend until she disappeared around the corner. Shaking her head, she hoped Marisa would get over whatever was bugging her, and soon.

Entering her tiny office, Marisha closed the door and leaned her back against it. She felt tired. She was sad, restless, and tired of being tired. "Something has to give," she thought. "I can't go on like this. My work is piling up, my friend is ready to disown me, and I do look like crap."

She was supposed to look glamorous, or at least elegant. Her job demanded it. After all, she was the top interior designer at Sadwick & Rockwell Inc. They paid her good money to go out and charm the rich and famous into signing a contract with their firm. How could she convince anyone that her designs would be fancy when she herself looked like something the cat had dragged in?

Walking towards her desk, she looked out the window. "Oh, for Christ's sake!" Angrily, she walked to the window and pulled the blind down. "How many times must I complain?" She was on the fourth floor of an office building and directly across the street was another office building. On several occasions, she'd noticed a man with a pair of binoculars, watching her window. He was also on the fourth floor. Marisha had ignored him for the first little while, but seeing him there day after day, it finally got to her. In a way, he was invading her privacy. She had already called security twice and each time they'd assured her that they'd look into it. "Well, whatever they were doing wasn't working, because there he was again!" she fumed.

Pushing the nosy neighbour out of her mind, Marisha sat down behind the desk, and forced herself to concentrate on work. She had phone calls to make, appointments to schedule and tons of data entry to deal with. Surprisingly, she managed to keep her mind on the tasks.

Five minutes before noon, her phone rang.

"Hello?" she answered.

"Hey. Are you ready to go?" Lilly's happy tone sounded fake.

"Is it lunch time already?" Marisha's voice reflected that she wasn't pleased with the interruption.

"Almost. Sorry to interrupt, but I just wanted to make sure you're not going to stand me up today," Lilly apologized.

"I'll be down in a couple of minutes," Marisha said and replaced the receiver. Since her wedding number three fiasco, she had neglected her friendship with Lilly. She felt guilty but was not able to do anything about it. She needed some time to get herself together and make peace with herself. Her friend meant well but Marisha was sure she wouldn't understand. How could she? Marisha herself didn't!

Shortly after noon, Marisha and Lilly walked to their favourite Italian pizzeria. For the past four years, they'd had lunch there almost every day. The cooks and the servers knew both women by their first names, and vice versa.

After ordering their meal, Lilly took out a bundle of papers from her purse.

"Well, here they are . . . our tickets. Man! I can't wait. Just think, in two short weeks, we'll be off to paradise."

"When did you pick those up?" Marisha asked.

"Yesterday, I had to go to the post office, and on the way back, I got a call from our travel agent that they were ready, so I picked them up," Lilly answered matter-of-factly.

"Why didn't you tell me this morning?"

"The pissy mood you were in, I didn't want to."

"I'm sorry Lilly. Lately, I can't sleep. I'm tired all the time . . . mornings are the worst."

"I've noticed." Lilly looked hurt.

"Lilly, I won't apologize again. Please put up with me for few more days. I'm sure things will get better," Marisha begged.

"OK. But promise me something."

"What?"

"Promise me that you won't take whatever is chewing at you to Mexico with us."

"I promise. We both need a holiday. We've waited a long time to do this. We'll have fun, no matter what," Marisha promised.

"I still wish you'd talk to me. It hurts that after all the years of our friendship you don't trust me enough to confide in me."

"It's not that I don't trust you, Lilly. I just can't talk about it, not yet."

Marisha took one pouch and examined the contents. Pulling out a colourful brochure, she waved it in front of Lilly's face.

"Two weeks of living like queens! Aqua waters, sunshine, and plenty of tequila! I'm so glad we chose that resort and went all-inclusive. Did you see the pictures of the place? They call it Tropical Palace for a reason. Look at it! It looks like a palace, and all those palm trees . . . and the beach!"

"Yeah, I checked out the brochure yesterday. It does look heavenly. And they have plenty of restaurants, bars, and even a disco joint right in the resort. Plenty of activities too. Check it out." Lilly pointed to the back page of the brochure. "Horses, parasailing, snorkelling—you name it, they've got it."

Eating their lunch and chatting about the great time they would have in Mexico relaxed the tension between them. They had been best friends since high school and until a few months ago, they had shared everything with one another. They lived in the same apartment block, worked in the same office building, and hung around with the same circle of friends. Marisha was a maid-of-honour at Lilly's wedding and she was there to hold her friend's hand when her husband was killed in a car accident five months later. Lilly was going to be Marisha's maid-of-honour, three times, but the weddings hadn't gone ahead. Until few months ago, they had not kept any secrets from one another. Marisha couldn't explain, even to herself, why she didn't share her latest problems with her best friend. She was hoping that once she had made peace with herself, she would be able to confide in Lilly. Months passed and she was still searching for answers. Marisha was fully aware of the strain she was putting on their friendship and she felt terrible about it.

After work, as soon as she'd finished cleaning up the dinner dishes, Marisha ran a hot bath. She fetched a glass of wine and her diary, and returned to the bathroom. The little room felt cozy and inviting. Inhaling the scent of tropical flowers from her favourite bubble bath, Marisha levered herself into the tub. Leaning back, she closed her eyes.

Silky white bubbles soothed her skin and the hot water relaxed her muscles, but her mind was racing. She tried to push the unwanted images away. It didn't work. She saw herself in a wedding dress, walking down the aisle. People were looking at her. Brian was standing at the altar, smiling, waiting. Then his smile was gone, replaced by surprise, disappointment, anger. She opened her eyes. "Jesus, will I ever stop thinking about it? Why must I relive this nightmare over and over?"

Taking a sip of her wine, she picked up the diary. Again, she studied the cover of the old scribbler. Its dark blue colour had faded to a light blue. As stained, wrinkled and faded as it was, it held the story of her past, of her beginning.

Sept. 22nd, 1974

Dear Diary,

Yesterday, I had a bad day with the kids. The two younger boys both woke up with a cold and the baby is teething. She has a runny nose, and I can feel a sharp tooth in her lower gums. Mark, the oldest, was being a brat. On top of that, my Aunt Helen came from the field with a nasty cut on her hand. Usually, as soon as I clean up after supper, I can come to my room, but last night I had to wash all the kids and put them to bed. Then I made lunches for my aunt and uncle for the next day. By the time I came to my room, I was very tired.

Today was a little better. The boys were playing together without fighting and crying, so I had more time to look after the baby. Auntie Helen's hand is better, too. Tonight, she was able to take care of the kids and the lunches.

Earlier today, I did something that I'm not very proud of. I read a letter addressed to my uncle. I've never done anything like this before. I know it was wrong, but I couldn't help it. A few days ago, a postman brought this letter. Since my uncle was in the field, I had to sign for it. The letter was from my Aunt Martha from Canada. In the evening, Uncle Lech read it and then left it on the shelf. When I was dusting this morning, I saw it and something told me to read it. Even though we're not supposed to read anyone else's mail, I'm glad I did.

I found out that both Auntie Martha and Uncle Joseph from Canada were sending money to Auntie Sonia. They were making sure that Auntie Sonia could afford to feed me and buy me clothes.

Something else too, Auntie Martha wants me to come and live with her in Canada. What do you think about that? She said that she's getting some papers prepared and as soon as they're ready, she'll send a plane ticket for me. I would like to know why no one is telling me about it.

I don't know what to think. I would love to go to Canada. They have cars, TVs, and nice houses. I know this because, with my school, I went on a field trip to a movie theatre once. We saw a movie about a teenage girl living in America. Gosh! She lived like a princess. We thought that it was all made up, but our teacher said that people really lived like that in the United States and in Canada. I can't even imagine myself living like that. Besides, I don't think I could go to Canada. Not on the plane, I'd be too scared. I'm mad at Aunt Sonia though. She always made me feel as though I was a big expense to her. I've given her all the money I earned, *she got money from Canada, and she never bought me clothes or anything. All the years I've lived with her, I got clothes from the ladies I worked for. Don't get me wrong, I appreciated them very much. I learned how to make them smaller, to fit me, and I have some nice outfits. The point is, if she got money from Canada, I think she should have told me. At least she could have bought me some shoes. I don't remember the last time I had shoes that fitted me. The ones I get from people are always too big or too small. Well, that's enough complaining for today. Talk to you tomorrow.*

Closing the book, Marisha shivered. "Now I know why I've become obsessed with buying shoes. Gosh! I remember how my feet always hurt. No wonder I have so many pairs of shoes in my closet now."

The water in the tub was barely warm. Marisha rinsed herself with a quick shower. Her head was filled with memories from her early years.

It was too early to go to sleep yet. "I'll get my pyjamas on, get into bed, and read some more," she decided. Just as she was getting into bed, the ringing of the phone brought her out of the bedroom and into the kitchen.

"Hello? Hello? I can hear you breathing, please who are you? What do you want from me?" Met with total silence, she replaced the phone on its cradle, and reached over to pull the cord from the jack. "I can't believe this! Lord! Why? Why me? I should've called the police!" She was hoping that after the last time when she had told the caller that she was going to the police, the calls would stop. Obviously, her threat hadn't scared the prankster away. For the past two months, every couple of days, someone had dialled her phone number and when she answered, the caller wouldn't talk. Positive that it was just some kids having fun at her expense, she didn't bother calling the police.

Pushing the prankster out of her thoughts, Marisha went back to the bedroom, settled in bed, and picked up her diary. Putting her reading glasses on, she found the page of the diary where she'd left off.

Sept. 28th, 1974

Dear Diary,

Today, I got a letter from Auntie Martha from Canada. It was addressed to me. You should see the beautiful stamps! I had to wait until the kids went for their naps before I could read it. I have never had a letter before. I was so excited! Auntie Martha asked me if I would like to come and live with her in Canada. Apparently, two years ago, she married this older Polish fellow, Ted, and since they had no children, they would like me to come and live with them. She says that Ted is a very nice man and that he loves children. She also said that I'd have my own room. She wants me to write to her and let her know how I feel about it. She says that my life would be much better in Canada.

I showed the letter to Auntie Helen. Auntie Helen thinks that I shouldn't have to think about it. There is nothing here in Poland for me and I should jump at the chance to get out. Aunt Helen also said that I should thank God that Auntie Martha wants to take me.

It's a big decision for me to make. I'm tired of looking after kids. Tired of living with different people every year, and tired of feeling as if I'm a burden to everyone. But this is the only life I know. What if I don't like Canada? What if Auntie Martha and her husband are mean to me?

Where would I go then? At least here, I have some family. There is always Aunt Sonia. Gosh! I'm scared.

Marisha wiped the tears from her eyes. She had been just a child then, so naïve and inexperienced. In the seventies, Poland was so far behind with everything, especially in the small villages. She was fifteen years old and had never seen a TV, never been on a plane or even sat in a car. She had made her own clothes and lived the life of a housewife, without having a house or a husband. "How did I do it? How did I survive?" With tears of self-pity running down her face, she picked up her diary again.

October 15th, 1974

Dear Diary,

Well, I did it. After thinking about it for a while, I wrote to Auntie Martha, and told her that I'd be happy to go to Canada.

I thought, why not? I really have nothing holding me back in Poland and going to Canada would be an adventure. If I don't like it maybe there will be a way for me to come back. I'll be eighteen soon and being of legal age, I'll be able to live my own life. If this Canada is as good as everyone makes it out to be, maybe I'll find a better life there. If not, I'll just come back to Poland somehow. I'm not sure about the plane though. I've never seen one up close, and I can't figure out how people can travel in it. It looks so small in the sky. How does it hang there without falling to the ground?

I asked Auntie Martha if there is any other way for me to get there, maybe by train or by bus. I think I have to cross the ocean though. I was never good at geography, so I'm not sure. I hope Auntie Martha will write soon.

The harvest is almost over. Auntie Helen spends more time at home now, so I don't have so much work to do. I look after the kids, but my auntie prepares meals and does the laundry. Uncle Lech still goes to the fields, but he comes home early.

From the old clothes I found in the attic, I've started making myself some outfits. If it really happens and I go to live with Auntie Martha, I will need something to wear. Auntie Helen is helping me. She said that she's surprised how good I am with a needle. Out of an old dress, I've made a skirt for her, and from smaller pieces, I'm making some outfits for the kids.

CHAPTER 3

D*EAR DIARY,*

I have some good news and some bad news. The good news is that I received a letter from Auntie Martha. She is happy that I decided to come to Canada. She is positive that I will love it there. She's getting my room ready. Doesn't that sound good?

The bad news is that to get there I have to go by plane or by boat. The boat will take almost a month to get there, so she said that I have to go on a plane. She also told me that I have to go back to Auntie Sonia's. She's closer to Warsaw and I'll have to make few trips to the Embassy building there. I'm excited and scared at the same time. Everything would be good if it wasn't for the plane.

I wrote to Auntie Sonia to let her know that I'll be coming back to her place at the end of November. Too bad I can't stay here. I like living with

Uncle Lech and Auntie Helen. I like the children too. I'll miss them all, but most of all, I'll miss my room.

I hope I won't have to work for Auntie Sonia's neighbours any more. Auntie Martha promised to send some money for my trips to Warsaw and some to buy clothes, so maybe I won't have to.

Uncle Lech gave me a ticket for the train today. He said that he and Auntie Helen appreciated all my help. He also promised to give me some money to go back with.

Dec. 19th, 1974

Dear Diary,

I just got back from Warsaw. Wow! I have never been to a big city before, and I have so much to tell you. Let me start from the beginning.

Back in November, Uncle Lech, Auntie Helen and all the children came to the train station to see me off. Just before the train left the station, Uncle Lech gave me some money and a present—a book about Canada.

The train ride was six hours long, but I didn't mind. I had to stand for the first two hours. Then some people got off and I found a seat. Finally, I could read the book. Looking at the pictures and reading about Canada, the hours just flew by. Canada is a very nice place. So big and clean, and people look happy. I think I'll like it there.

When I arrived at Lipa, Auntie Sonia was waiting for me at the train station. Imagine my surprise when she told me that she was glad to see me. I wanted to give her a hug but she backed away.

Back at the apartment, I was putting my things away and Aunt Sonia was warming up some soup. She was very talkative. She asked me if I really wanted to go to Canada. I told her that I did. Then she said that it wasn't a good idea for me to go that far away. She complained about being old and sick, and not having anyone to look after her. She thought that I should stay with her.

After having my own space in the attic, the thought of living in this tiny, mouldy apartment and sharing that thing called a bed with her reassured me that I was doing the right thing. Canada was looking really good.

Later that week, we got a letter from Auntie Martha. She sent some money and told us that we had to go to Warsaw to apply for a passport.

Auntie Sonia started again with the complaints about her old age and frail health. She looked pretty healthy to me—skinny, but healthy. She just didn't want to go to Warsaw, that's all. It took the next-door neighbour to convince her that she had to go with me because I was a minor and she was my legal guardian. That did the trick.

I had to get my picture taken for the passport. That was exciting. I got dressed up nicely and even curled my hair.

The photographer sat me on a chair and told me to pinch my cheeks. I felt silly doing it, but he said that everybody did it.

When the pictures were ready, I went to pick them up. At first, I wasn't sure if I liked them. Now, I think they're not bad.

Then came the day we had to leave for Warsaw. Lord! I thought I'd have to carry Auntie Sonia onto the train. She was sure that she wouldn't survive the trip. I kept talking to her all the way, trying to keep her distracted. When we got off the train, she crossed herself and for a moment, I thought that she'd fall to her knees and kiss the ground. I'm not sure, but I think she's scared of trains.

Then it was my turn to get scared. I knew that Warsaw was a big city but I didn't know what to expect. Coming out of the train station, I had to stop. There were so many people, cars and big buildings, I was scared to move. Auntie Sonia had to pull me by my hand or I'd still be standing there.

Walking down the sidewalks, I saw store windows with plastic people wearing beautiful clothes, and windows full of shoes and books and toys. It was just like in America. On the road, I saw funny looking buses; Auntie Sonia said they were trolleys. They looked so weird. And the cars! So many of them, and they were going so fast! I felt dizzy.

Then we walked by the palace! A real palace! It was big and beautiful, and had lots of statues all around it. Auntie said that it was a museum. I wanted to go and see it up close but she said that we had no time.

We went into a huge building. There were so many people in there we had to stand in a line-up for over an hour. When our turn came, we went up to a little window. There was a woman there. She looked mad or something. We gave her my birth certificate and my pictures. She asked us a whole lot of questions and then said that someone would let us know if my application for a passport is approved. I don't know what that meant but Auntie Sonia thanked her and we left. Before we got back on the train, Auntie went into her fits again. I asked her if she was scared of the train. She told me not to be silly, that she was just very sick and instead of running around the country, she should be at home in her bed. When I asked her if she liked Warsaw, she told me that she had been there before; didn't like it then, and she didn't like it now. "Too many people . . . always in a hurry to go nowhere . . . nothing good about the city folk . . . look how the women dress, how they paint their faces. No, I'm glad I live in a village . . . it's safer," she told me.

Well, I don't care what she says; I think Warsaw is a beautiful city. I love the old, fancy buildings and the streets lined with huge trees on both sides. In the villages, where I usually stay, the houses are all the same: four *walls, windows, and a roof. In Warsaw, almost every house is different. Buildings are much bigger and taller, have lots of windows, and each is different from the other. Some have big verandas in front; some even have pillars holding small roofs over the doors. I wonder what it would be like to live in a city. I think I'd like it.*

From the train, I could see more of the city. And I saw Wisla! In school I learned a poem about this river. The poem said that Wisla looks like a blue ribbon running through Poland. It does look like a ribbon. Maybe one day I'll be able to go back and spend some time in Warsaw. I would like to do that.

This waiting is hard for me. I wish they'd give me the passport. I don't know how long it will take but I'm getting bored. I don't have anything to do right now. With no school, and no work, I just sit and watch Auntie Sonia embroider and listen to her complaining. She's lecturing me too. She thinks that I should stay in Poland. Going to Canada, in her opinion, is not for people like me. Nothing good will come of it, she says. She's heard somewhere that Canada is a wild country. She is positive that most of the people there are sinners. "God doesn't live in Canada," she told me. Oh well, Auntie Martha lives there and she likes it. It can't be all that bad.

As soon as I get the passport, I'm supposed to let Auntie Martha know. Until then, all I can do is wait.

Dec. 26th, 1974

Dear Diary,

Once again, I spent Christmas with Auntie Sonia. It was just the two of us. As always, it was pretty sad. Our tiny Christmas tree is the poorest thing you've ever seen. Auntie Sonia doesn't think we should throw money away on unnecessary things.

She gave me a Christmas present this year. I was very surprised. She's never given me anything before. Right after dinner, she came up to me and handed me a white bundle. "Here. Something to remember me by," she said.

It was the embroidery she had been working on for the past few weeks—a beautiful, snow-white tablecloth with a colourful border of wild flowers. I know I'll cherish this present forever. When I get married, it will be on my Christmas table every year and hopefully I'll be able to pass it on to my children. I felt bad for not getting anything for her. It would be nice to give her something to remember me, too. I promised myself that I'd send her something from Canada.

Listening to the noises coming from our building, I wonder what it would be like to have a family. If my mom and dad were alive, what would our Christmases be like?

Our neighbours were cooking and cleaning for days because their children or their relatives were coming. Now they are singing, laughing and talking. I think our apartment is the quietest of them all.

When I get married, I'll have a houseful of kids. I'll invite Auntie Martha and Uncle Joseph and we'll be singing, laughing and talking too.

But first, I need that passport!

CHAPTER 4

ENTERING HER OFFICE, Marisha noticed that the "spy" in the next building was looking into her window again. Picking up the phone, she dialled security.

"Hi, this is Marisha Pawlak. What's the story on the guy next door?"

Randy Selleck, a fifty-something security guard, answered her call.

"Good Morning, Miss Pawlak. We did make some inquiries. The window you pointed out is in an empty office. No one has seen anyone coming or going from there."

"Well, he's there right now. Why don't you go and check it out, please. I don't like to be spied on every morning." Marisha's tone left no room for arguments.

"We'll see what we can do," Randy promised.

"Thank you."

Marisha hung up the phone. She thought, "If that's an empty office, then the man with the binoculars must be going there with the purpose of spying on me, but why? What can he learn from looking into my window? It's not as though I'm holding secret meetings or hanging secret maps on the walls. So what is he after?" A soft knock on the door startled her out of her thoughts.

"Come in," she cried.

A serious young man of about twenty-five poked his head through the doorway.

"Miss Pawlak?"

"Yes."

"I have a delivery for you." The young man came towards Marisha and handed her a vase with a dozen yellow roses. Without waiting for a tip, he quickly made his exit.

Nervously, Marisha looked for a card. The last time she'd received yellow roses there had been no card. It was fun thinking about some secret admirer sending her flowers. That was then. Now she was spied on, someone was making prank calls to her home and it wasn't fun anymore.

Finding no envelope attached to the bouquet, Marisha shoved the flowers into the wastebasket, vase and all. "Who is doing this to me? And why?" She felt a cold chill run down her spine. Taking a quick look out of the window, she noticed that the spy was gone. "Could the calls and the flowers be from the same person, the one spying on me, or do I have a procession of people waiting in line to make my life miserable?" Either way, it was beyond her why anyone would bother with her. She wasn't rich or famous. "Oh well, maybe the security will come up with something this time." She was hopeful.

Pulling out some files, Marisha forced herself to concentrate on work. It took some doing, but eventually she managed to forget the prank calls, the yellow roses, and the man with the binoculars.

At noon, Lilly called to remind her that it was lunchtime but Marisha declined the invitation to go out. She wasn't hungry today and she had too much work to deal with. Lilly wasn't happy with her brush off.

"Look kid, you have to eat. Come on, let's go for a walk. We can grab a hotdog or a burger for a change. What do you say?" she asked.

"Please Lilly, don't be mad at me, but I really can't go today. I'll make it up to you, I promise."

"Fine, have it your way." Lilly hung up.

Marisha stared at the dead phone in her hand. "I'll make it up to you, I promise," she repeated in a hushed voice and replaced the receiver.

In the afternoon, on her way to a meeting, Marisha paused by Lilly's desk. Lilly was looking at her computer screen, her fingers flying over the keyboard.

"Sorry about lunch. Where did you eat?" Marisha asked.

Lilly stopped typing, but her eyes didn't leave the computer screen. "Nowhere. I'm in a middle of something. I'll talk to you later, OK?" she muttered.

Marisha opened her mouth to apologize again but changed her mind. "OK, take care," she said instead.

Sitting in a taxi thinking about Lilly turned Marisha's mood from bad to worse. She didn't blame Lilly for giving her the cold shoulder because she'd deserved it. If Lilly treated her the way she treated Lilly, Marisha didn't think she'd be as patient as her friend was. Shaking her head, she thought about how her private life was affecting her work and her friendship with Lilly. "I have to make some changes and quickly, before it's too late!"

The meeting with a potential client didn't go well at all. Marisha blamed herself for not being able to present her proposal with confidence and enthusiasm, the way she would have in the past. The man had left the meeting with, "I'll let you know." In her line of work it most often meant, "Thanks, but no thanks."

Returning to the office building, she walked past Lilly's desk and again her friend ignored her. Frustrated, Marisha continued towards her office. "I need to get away from everything and everyone, even for a couple of days," she decided. Waiting two weeks for Mexico was too long and besides, she wouldn't be alone there and she needed to be alone.

Requesting two days off, just before she took two weeks' vacation, wasn't going to look good, but she had no choice. What good was she if she couldn't concentrate on her job? What was the point of going to her appointments if she couldn't land the contracts? Making up her mind, she phoned her supervisor and requested to see him.

One look at Marisha and Jim Barnes knew that something was bothering his favourite employee. She didn't have that "Listen to me, I know what I'm talking about," aura about her. Today she looked and sounded wishy-washy, to say the least. This was a busy time for the company and he was giving her two weeks off at the end of the month. Yet how can he refuse her? It was not as though she asked for days off all the time.

"The best I can do for you would be the rest of today and tomorrow," Jim offered.

"Thank you, sir. I appreciate it." Disappointment was clearly visible on Marisha's face. Jim felt bad but he couldn't afford to let her go for two whole days. He had Matson waiting for the final presentation and there was no one better than Marisha to convince the man to take the deal. Matson was picky and stubborn, but Miss Pawlak would find a way to get through to him. She knew how to talk to people like Matson.

Arriving home, Marisha checked her answering machine. Finding no messages, she unplugged the phone. "I'm going to pretend that I'm not home," she said to herself.

She fixed a light meal and decided to spend the evening reading her diary. Tomorrow, she'd have a whole day to think about her problems and hopefully she'd come to some sort of conclusion. Today, she was mad at herself and mad at the whole world. There was no point trying to figure out anything now. The mood she was in, she wouldn't get very far, anyway.

The moment the kitchen was cleaned up, she took a blanket and her diary into the living room. Curling up on the sofa, she started reading.

Jan. 18th, 1975

Dear Diary,

Finally, today, I got the passport. I had no idea what it would look like, and I was surprised to see a little book. I don't know what I was expecting. The passport is small but it looks very impressive. With my picture on the first page, I feel important just holding it.

Auntie Sonia has been very discouraging in the past couple of weeks. She's repeatedly told me that the Polish government wouldn't let me out of the country, that I'd better start thinking about finding a job, and stop dreaming about going to Canada. She even told me that I was stupid for thinking that the government would give me a passport. "Why would they bother with the likes of you? You are nobody, and they have better things to do with their time," she told me. God! I hate her for talking like that, but I had a feeling. I knew that I would get the passport. Why would the government want to keep me here, anyway? I'm not important or famous; they don't need me for anything.

Anyway, I've got it. She wouldn't even look at it! Can you believe it?

I wrote to Auntie Martha right away. I'm so excited. I don't know how long it will take, but I think I'll be in Canada before the summer. Aunt Sonia tells me not to count my chickens. She still thinks that I won't go.

My mind is made up. I'm going!

Feb. 17th, 1975

Dear Diary,

Now all I need is a plane ticket, but nothing from Auntie Martha yet. I'm waiting for the mailman every day, and when I see him, every day he shakes his head, "No." He knows what I'm waiting for.

I have to tell you something. On the third floor of our apartment building, there is this girl. She makes fun of me, calls me "America." I really don't like her. A couple of months ago, I was coming back from the store and she stopped me in the hallway and asked why I don't go to school.

I told her that I would be going to Canada soon and didn't need to go to school. She didn't believe me. From that day, every time she sees me, she laughs at me and calls me "America."

I don't care. Soon, she'll see that I'm telling the truth. Until then, I avoid her. Our next-door neighbour, Mr. Kawczyk, doesn't believe me either. He told me once that it's not so easy to get out of Poland. I showed him my passport. He was surprised, but he doesn't think that I'll actually go. He and Aunt Sonia make a perfect pair. She, too, thinks that I'm living in a dream world.

Feb. 26th, 1975

Dear Diary,

Don't have much to write about. Nothing is happening. Every day is the same. The biggest news since my passport came is the letter Aunt Sonia got from Uncle Joseph from Canada. He sent some money and asked Aunt Sonia to take me shopping for whatever I needed. He told us that Auntie Martha was having some problems with my plane ticket, but she was working on it, and would send it as soon as she could.

Aunt Sonia didn't want to take me shopping, but she gave me some money to buy a suitcase and new undies. What I really need are shoes!

In Lipa, we have only one store. You can buy everything from hoes to sewing needles, pots, and fabric, to clothes and rubber boots, but no shoes. For shoes, you have to go to Starnole, a small town about forty kilometres from here. I would love to go there, but Aunt Sonia refuses to come with me and she won't let me go alone. I don't understand why. I'm not a baby! I've been on a train many times by myself. Soon, I'll go to a different country all by myself, so why can't I go alone on a bus or a train to a town forty kilometres away?

My old shoes are so worn out and ugly, I hate the thought of wearing them to Canada. I've tried painting them, but it didn't help much. Oh well, I can't do anything about it, so I'll just have to get used to the idea that my first steps in Canada will be taken in a pair of very ugly shoes.

I love my suitcase though. It's not really a suitcase, just a bag, but it is so nice and new. I love new things; they smell so nice. My bag is not very big, but since I don't have much to put into it, and I'll have to carry it, it's perfect. At the store, they had this bag in two colours, brown and blue. I took the blue one.

Auntie Sonia had a conniption when she found out how much I had to pay for it. She called me a fool. She said that I would never amount to anything if I didn't watch my money. Oh well, who cares? She hates everything I do, anyway.

I wrote a letter to Uncle Joseph and thanked him for the money. I can't wait to meet him and Auntie Martha, they both sound so nice.

I wonder what my parents would think if they knew I was going to Canada. Especially my dad, what would he say if he knew that I was going to live with his older sister?

March 17th, 1975

Dear Diary,

At last! The mailman came to our door today. He gave me a letter from Auntie Martha, and asked me to sign for it.

I got the plane ticket! I danced around the apartment for fifteen minutes. I was so happy. Auntie Sonia thought that I'd lost my mind.

I couldn't help it. I'm going to Canada!!!!

I have to be at the Warsaw International Airport, on April 27th at two o'clock in the afternoon. My flight leaves at 3:20.

Aunt Sonia cried when I showed her the ticket. She said that she's worried about me going that far, all by myself. I read her Auntie Martha's letter to reassure her that the family will meet me at the airport, but it just made things worse. She mentioned the plane, and how dangerous it was and that got me going. At first, I tried not to think about it, but it didn't work. I think about it every second, and my stomach is turning. How on earth am I going to get on that plane?

It would be nice if Aunt Sonia said something reassuring to me but just hearing the word "plane," she crosses herself. She says that the devil himself invented this contraption to lure people to their death. She told me that flying in a plane is against God's will. "If God intended us to fly, he'd give us wings," she told me.

I tried to reason with her that we hear and see planes flying in the sky every day. There must be people on them; maybe it's not as bad as we think. I also told her to look at it this way, that if I'm meant to live in Canada, I'll get there safely; if it's not meant to be, then there isn't much I can do about it. She told me that there was something I could do. "You could stay away from the plane, stay here, and help your old aunt. With your luck, you'll find no happiness in a strange land."

I did ask her what she meant by "my luck" but she just waved her hand and hissed like a cat.

There is no way to get through to her! I think she's going strange.

I have to write a letter to Auntie Martha tomorrow and let her know that I got the ticket and that I'll be on the plane.

There is plenty of time for me to work up the courage to go on the plane. I just hope I'll stop being so scared.

Marisha closed the book. Pressing it to her chest, she was glad that she'd kept it. At the time, it was just someone, or rather, something, to share her thoughts with, a way for her to voice her fears and her concerns. Now, it was a passage to her past. Every feeling, every emotion she had written in this book all those years ago came back to her, vivid and fresh, as if it had happened just yesterday. She could laugh at herself now, but she remembered how terrified she had been that day and how unreasonable Aunt Sonia had been about the whole thing.

The memories brought a sad little smile to Marisha's lips. With that same smile, she woke up at 4:30 am. "Gosh, I fell asleep. I can't believe I've slept for six hours!"

Getting up from the sofa, she picked up her diary and the blanket and went to the bedroom. Amazingly, she still felt tired.

As she crawled into bed, her thoughts went back to Poland and Aunt Sonia's apartment but the visit wasn't long because she fell asleep again.

CHAPTER 5

THE RELUCTANT RINGING of the phone woke Marisha out of a deep sleep.

"Hello?" she managed sleepily.

"Marisha, are you still sleeping?"

"Oh . . . hi, Lilly, yeah, you woke me up."

"But it's almost nine o'clock! You're late!"

"Late for what?" Marisha was confused.

"For work, silly!"

"No. I took the day off today."

"That's nice. Thanks for telling me," Lilly said sarcastically.

"It was a last-minute decision, sorry," Marisha said apologetically.

"And what . . . you couldn't phone me at home?"

"Sorry."

"That's all I hear from you lately. 'Sorry Lilly, I'm so sorry Lilly.' What the hell? Are we still friends or not?" Lilly exploded.

"Don't be silly, of course we are, and you know it. Hey, why don't you come over for dinner tonight? I'll even cook. No take-out, OK?" Marisha offered guiltily.

"What time?" Lilly's voice softened a little.

"Whenever, I'll be home all day."

"Are you feeling OK?"

"Yeah. I've got some things to work out, I'll be fine, I promise."

"OK. I'll be there about, hmmm . . . six."

"See you at six, and Lilly, have a good one, hey?"

"Thanks, you too . . . see ya." Lilly hung up.

Not wanting to get out of bed just yet, Marisha stretched lazily, fluffed up the pillows, and made herself comfortable. Pulling the covers up to her chin, she thought how nice it was to have the opportunity to laze around. This was the first night in two months that she had slept right through. She needed that sleep desperately. She felt happier this morning, happier and stronger. "It was a good idea to take a day off," she thought. Closing her eyes, she enjoyed the cozy warmth of her bed.

Brian came to mind, but Marisha pushed him away. "I'm not ready to tackle this one yet. I need coffee first." She knew she had to deal with the Brian issue today. It was time to face the facts and move on with her life. Lilly had to be dealt with, too. For the past two months, her best friend had put up with a lot from her; there was no excuse for torturing her any longer.

Looking at the nightstand, she spied her diary. "Oh well, my problems can wait another hour or two."

She reached over and picked up the book.

April 27th, 1975

Dear Diary,

Well, here I am—at the International Airport in Warsaw. I didn't think I'd be writing until I got to Canada, but I can't stay still. I've tried reading a magazine, but I couldn't concentrate.

I had to get up very early this morning to catch the train to Warsaw. Aunt Sonia didn't want to come with me. I begged and begged, but she wouldn't budge. I was scared to come by myself, but I had no choice.

From the train, I was going to walk to the airport, but I didn't know which way to go. I asked a man for directions and he told me that it was too far to walk. He said that I'd have to take a taxi. Boy! I had no idea how to take a taxi. I knew that it was a car with a sign "taxi" on it, but how on earth was I going to find one? The man told me to go back and wait in front of the train station. "Sooner or later, a taxi will show up there," he told me.

Sure enough, a few minutes after I got back there, a nice shiny taxi stopped right in front of me. Let me tell you, I felt so stupid, I didn't know how to open the door! The man had to come out and open it for me. He laughed at me when I apologized and told him that I had never been in a car before.

I must say, I didn't like the ride at all. I felt sick to my stomach. Thank God I didn't throw-up. I felt like it, but I didn't. We were going so fast! I was scared!

When we got to the airport, I had to give the taxi man most of my money. Aunt Sonia would have a bird if she knew how much I had to pay!

Then I had to go inside the airport. I didn't know what to expect and of course I was scared.

Well, to tell the truth, it wasn't too bad. There were some line-ups inside, so I stood in one of them. When I got to the counter, a nice-looking woman asked me for my ticket. I showed it to her and told her that I was going to Canada. After looking at my ticket, she called someone on the phone and a man came and took me to another counter. He looked at my ticket, took my bag, and showed me where I had to go.

I'm worried though, because when he took my ticket, he ripped something out of it. I hope it wasn't important. I'm sure Auntie Martha paid good money for this ticket. What will she say when she sees pieces of it missing? Not only that, but he took my new bag away, too. He said that I'll get it back in Canada.

"With all the people there, how will they know that this bag is mine?" I asked him. He told me not to worry, and give me two little pieces of paper. He said that one was for my bag, and the other was a boarding pass. I had no idea what that was all about.

When I went through the door he sent me to, there was another line-up! It's just like going to the grocery store after the delivery truck leaves—line-ups everywhere. Anyway, I couldn't see anything for a while. When I came to the front, I was told to walk through a funny looking gateway, I don't know why. There was plenty of room to go around it, but two people dressed in dark clothes insisted that we all went through that gate, one at a time. Some people even had to take off their jackets and put them on the counter. I'm not positive, but I think I saw the woman behind that counter put her hand into the pocket of one jacket. She was dressed like a police officer, but she couldn't be. I've never heard of women police.

Now I'm sitting in a plastic chair, in a room full of people. I was looking out of the window for a while, but watching the planes come and go made me very nervous again.

I watched some people getting off the plane. There were so many of them! I don't know how they all fitted in there.

There are lots of people waiting with me; I hope that not all of them will go on the same plane as me, especially this big man. Gosh! He is huge! I really don't think he'll fit inside the plane.

There are a few small kids with their parents and men in suits and nice looking ladies. Everyone is just sitting reading or looking out of the window. Even the kids don't seem to be worried. I think that I'm the only person here that is so scared.

Oh good, the fat man just left. Another plane came in. My stomach doesn't feel very good right now. I'm glad I took my diary out of my bag. Writing keeps me busy, and now and then, I forget how scared I am. Rats! The fat man is back.

Got to go, everybody is standing up and they're going to the little desk. Oh my God! Oh my God! I'm inside the plane. It looks almost like a train, but the seats are fancier and the windows are smaller. It smells nicer too.

Just as I got in, some woman took the piece of paper, that boarding pass, from me and she showed me where to sit. She didn't give me back the boarding pass. I hope I won't need it later.

To my horror, the fat man came in too. He went to the back of the plane. I don't think this will work. Too much weight in the back, I mean.

The woman came back and told me to wear a belt. I can't pull it out. It's stuck to the chair. I'm holding it in my hand. I'm hoping she won't notice.

I had to stop writing for a while. The plane started to move. We were going slowly at first. It was fun. Then we stopped. I thought that something was wrong, because we were just sitting there for a while.

Then we started to go again. This time we went faster. Then the plane turned around. I thought that we were going back to the airport. I was wrong.

When the plane turned around, it went faster and faster. It was going faster than a train. I felt the front of the plane lift off the ground. I was so scared that I closed my eyes. The front stayed up, but the back end of the plane was still down. I knew it! It had trouble lifting the fat man!

When I got brave enough to open my eyes, I looked out the window. We were up in the air, but the back of the plane was still lower than the front.

I was sure that we'd fly all the way to Canada like that because of that big man. I wonder why they didn't put him more in the middle.

It didn't take too long before the plane straightened out. Now I don't feel anything. It doesn't even feel like we're moving.

Shortly after we left the ground, my ears plugged up and I felt a horrible pain in my head. I was ready to scream, but my ears popped. I have never felt a pain like that.

The plane woman came to me and told me that I can take off my belt. I don't want her to know that it is broken, so I'm keeping it on. I don't know how long I'll be on this plane.

It's kind of nice, flying like this. I see that there are a few women working on this plane. They are called stewardesses. They were giving something to everyone. I hoped that they'd give me something too. They did. I've got a cute little tray, with beautiful white plastic plates filled with food. I had no idea what it was, but it smelled good, and tasted awesome. *I wish I could have kept the dishes, but the stewardess took the whole tray away.*

She gave me a drink too, a bottle of Coca Cola. I saw the little black bottles in the store in Warsaw, but I've never tasted one before. It didn't look like much; all black like coffee, but wow, did it taste good!

I see people going into a small door at the front of the plane. There was even a line-up there once. I wonder why they go in there. They don't stay long. Even the fat man went in there. I was surprised that he fitted through the little door!

Boy! Do I feel stupid! I had to go to the little door too. It's a bathroom! Who would've known that they'd have a bathroom on the plane?

When the stewardess asked me if I needed the bathroom, I told her no. Then she pointed out the little door up front, "in case you need it later," she told me.

As scared as I was to get out of my seat, I was very curious what a bathroom would look like here, on a plane. Amazing! Even the toilet is fancy, running water and all, but there was no way I could use it.

The stewardesses are walking around with candy and magazines. I got some too. Why not? They were giving them to everyone.

Aunt Sonia would have a stroke if she saw me now, sitting on a plane, eating candy and reading a magazine. Well, not really reading. The print is in English, I think, but the pictures are nice.

I tried to read some lines, but it looks very hard. How am I going to learn English? First things first, how are we going to get back on the ground?

Lord! If I ever get to Canada, I'll never go on the plane again! While I was trying to read my English magazine, the stewardess came back and told me to put my seat belt on again. She said that we were going to land.

The front of the plane tilted down and it stayed that way for a while. Then I saw the ground. Man! Was I scared! I thought we were going to crash into the houses below.

When the wheels touched the ground, the plane jumped. I screamed! But shortly, we were safely driving on a road. Once the plane stopped, people started to get off. I followed one group. We left the plane and got on a big bus. I sat at the very back. There was a woman up front. She was talking on the microphone, but I couldn't understand a word she was saying.

All the heads in front of me were turning left and right. I looked out of the windows; there was nothing special to see. Some old buildings, lots of cars and streetcars, that's it. The people on the bus were very interested in everything. Then we drove by a big castle. It was beautiful, not as beautiful as the one I saw in Warsaw, but it was nice.

Then we came back to the airport, and everyone lined up at the counter again. When my turn came, the woman behind the counter asked me something. I didn't understand what she wanted. I told her that I had come to Canada and I had to find my Auntie Martha. To prove it, I showed her my passport. She phoned someone and a man came. The man and the woman talked to each other and to me. I didn't understand anything. Then the man took me by the hand and pulled me with him. I was scared.

We went into a small room. He looked at my passport again and called someone on a little radio. Next, another man came in. I think that one was a policeman. The policeman stayed with me and the other man went somewhere.

God! Was I scared! I think I was crying. Where is my Auntie Martha? What did those men want with me?

The first man came back and he brought another man with him. The policeman left. To my relief, the new man spoke Polish.

He asked me so many questions that I got all mixed up. I tried to tell him that I had come to Canada to live with my Auntie Martha, but he just shook his head. He told me to stop crying and demanded that I tell him the truth.

I got mad at him. Why did he think I was making everything up? I decided not to say anything any more. What's the point?

Once I stopped talking, he asked to see my passport and my ticket. I didn't want to show it to him. I didn't trust him. Then he got mad at me. He asked me if I was running away. I just looked at him.

All of a sudden, he turned nice. He said that I was in a lot of trouble and if I wanted him to help me, I'd have to talk to him. Why would I be in trouble? I didn't need his help!

Once again, I explained to him why I had come to Canada. Boy! Was I surprised when he told me that I was not in Canada but in London! He said that I was supposed to stay on the plane and carry on to Canada. When the stewardess noticed that I wasn't on the plane, everyone had been looking for me. Naturally, they thought that I had run away. Can you believe it? Run away from what?

Then the man asked me, "If you're not running away, why did you leave the airport?" Well, I told him that I just followed the people. They got on the bus, so I did too.

He told me that I went on a tour of London with a tour group from Sweden. No wonder I couldn't understand a word they were saying!

He checked my ticket and told me that my plane left three hours ago and the next one wouldn't be leaving for another five hours. He wanted to know if I had Auntie Martha's phone number. I don't know if she even has a phone in her house. I don't know anyone who has a phone in their house.

My poor aunt will be so worried when the plane comes to Canada without me on it. The man said that I could have a problem getting a seat on the next plane. Things didn't look very good for me. Then he said something into his little radio and the policeman came back to the room. The Polish man said that he'd go and see about the next plane to Canada, and Joe (the policeman) will take me to get something to eat. I said that I wasn't hungry, but he told me not to argue and do as I was told.

I walked beside Joe through the airport. Man! That place was huge! I couldn't believe that we were inside. And the people! I don't think I've ever seen so many people in one place. I had so many questions, but Joe didn't speak Polish, so I couldn't ask him.

He took me to a restaurant and left me sitting at a small table. From the gesture he made, I understood that he wanted me to sit and not move. When he came back, he brought me a funny looking bun with some meat inside. Everything was perfectly round, the bun, the meat; even the little seeds on top of the bun were round. It tasted different; I can't explain, just different. And I had another Coca Cola. I really liked that. Joe had coffee; he didn't eat anything.

Then the Polish man came back and took me to another room with those funny gates. This time there were three gates side-by-side. He said that I was going on the next plane, but I had to wait two hours. He also told me that once I went through security, I couldn't leave. He gave me back my passport and my ticket.

I went through the gate, but I didn't see any security. I sat in a chair for two hours, just looking out of the window. I didn't want to miss the next plane.

I am so tired that I didn't even get scared when I got onto this plane. I didn't even care that this one was bigger and heavier looking than the last one. I need a bathroom and some sleep, but I don't think I can do either.

Where is Canada? I've been flying for so many hours already! Anyway, I don't even feel like writing any more.

Getting out of bed, Marisha smiled and shook her head. "That was some adventure. I can't believe how dumb I was back then." But really, how could she not be? Born and raised in a village, living with Aunt Sonia, where would she learn about the real world? She never saw much past her front and back yard. Going to Warsaw couple of times was always a fast trip, so she had no chance to see anything.

Reliving her simple existence through her diary made her sad, but at the same time, it was an eye opener. She thought, "How quickly we get spoiled. We take everything for granted; get used to better life, and very quickly we forget that it wasn't always like that. How many times do I get ticked off because I can't decide what to wear? I should be singing with joy that I have choices!"

Finishing her shower and morning toiletries, Marisha's head was still filled with memories of her trip to Canada. Until she read her diary, she had never thought about that time, that important step that had changed her life, forever.

CHAPTER 6

P ROMISING LILLY A home-cooked meal was one thing, but actually preparing it was almost impossible. Last time Marisha had cooked a full dinner was more than two months ago for Brian. Since then, she had lived on take-out and instant dinners.

Pushing the boxes of frozen TV dinners around the freezer compartment of her fridge, she was hoping to find something that could be turned into a nice entrée. Not seeing anything of interest, she shut the freezer door. "Looks like I have to make a trip to the store. Shoot! Why did I offer to cook? Today of all days!" But the offer was made, and since cancelling it was not an option, Marisha had no choice but to get dressed and go to the market.

Within an hour, she was back with three bags full of groceries.

She always enjoyed cooking, even in Poland where the food was scarce and the meals were very simple. Food there was more for survival, not like here. In Canada, everything was prepared to appeal not only to the taste buds, but also to the eye. Learning to use a variety of flavours and spices took time, but eventually she had mastered the art of gourmet cooking.

Cleaning the salad greens, Marisha let her mind wonder to the time she was preparing dinner for her first boyfriend, Greg. She had met him when she was still in high school. He was her first love and she thought that he would be her only love.

Greg lived on the same street as Aunt Martha. Marisha literally ran into him at the park. She'd had another episode with Uncle Ted and wanted to get as far away from him as possible, so she'd stormed out of the house. With anger and tears blinding her vision, she'd rounded the gate of the park and knocked a young man off his feet. He grabbed her arm for support and, in the process, pulled her to the ground with him. Greg hit the cement first and Marisha landed on top of him. After the initial shock wore off, they both burst out laughing. They sat there for some time, Marisha apologizing and Greg assuring her that, other than his pride, nothing else was hurt. Helping each other to their feet, they made their way to a bench. One thing led to another and after taking a stroll through the park and making a date for the following day, Greg walked her home.

He was tall and handsome and Marisha had lost herself in his beautiful blue eyes. From that day, he'd become her whole life. She was in love.

Of course, Uncle Ted was outraged. Auntie Martha wasn't too pleased either.

That was a long time ago, yet Marisha remembered how good it felt to be so happy and so in love. She had tried her best to convince her guardians that Greg was the one for her. When all her attempts failed, she threatened that with or without their blessing, she was going to date Greg and one day she'd marry him.

So what happened? Why didn't she marry him? They were in love, wedding plans were made . . .

The memories of her "almost marriage" made Marisha irritable. Tossing the salad with more force than was necessary, she sent some leaves onto the counter and to the floor. Looking at the mess she'd made, she leaned against the counter and hung her head. "Great, just great!" she thought miserably.

Abandoning her task, she poured herself a cup of coffee and walked to the living room. "Okay, I need to think about Greg, Roman and Brian, and about what happened, or I won't be able to do anything."

Sipping her coffee, she forced her memory back to the time she had moved out on her own. It was two weeks after her eighteenth birthday; she and Lilly were working as waitresses at the restaurant. Thomas Wilson was a cook there. Thomas owned a twelve-suite apartment block next to the restaurant.

One evening, when they all sat down for their coffee break, Thomas was complaining about one of his tenants moving out without giving him proper notice. Marisha complained about her uncle, and Lilly was positive that if she stayed in her parents' house one more day, she'd murder her younger brother in cold blood! Jokingly, Thomas suggested that Lilly and Marisha could rent his vacant apartment. The girls laughed at first, but the idea was planted and, like a seed, it started to grow. The more they talked about it, the more they liked the idea. They were of legal age now;

the apartment was next to their work; and between the two of them, they'd have no problem paying the rent. A week later, they signed a one-year lease.

That same year, Greg asked Marisha to marry him. He was twenty years old, had a well-paying job in the construction industry and was ready to settle down. They loved each other, and since they'd spent every available minute together anyway, why not do it as husband and wife? Marisha agreed to marry him, but she wanted to wait until the following year. She'd be nineteen then.

Greg bought a little house and begged Marisha to move in with him but she insisted that they wait until they were married. She loved the little house and looked forward to living there, but she knew her aunts and uncles would be horrified if she lived with Greg before they got married.

Thinking about it now, Marisha realized that she was using her family as an excuse. They hadn't spoken to her since she'd moved into the apartment and obviously they didn't care what she did or where she lived. Furthermore, if she were honest with herself, she'd admit that she had stopped caring what they thought a long time before that.

"Maybe, down deep inside," she thought, "I knew back then that marrying Greg would be a mistake. Then why did I agree to marry him? Was it because my family was against it?" Whatever the reason, the wedding plans were being put into action.

At that time, Lilly was seriously involved with Nathan. They had known each other for over a year and the plan was that after Marisha's wedding, Nathan was to move in with Lilly and take over Marisha's lease.

Every detail was worked out; everything was taken care of. Greg's parents made all the necessary arrangements for the nuptials.

Two months before the wedding, Marisha woke up sweat-drenched and frightened. She'd had a strange dream. In it, her mother and father were forbidding her marriage to Greg. They were so angry! They took turns yelling at her and calling her ugly names. The dream seemed very real and it hurt and frightened her terribly. For weeks, she struggled to push the dream out of her thoughts, but her efforts failed. The image of her parents' angry faces spoiled her days and haunted her nights. Seeking comfort and reassurance, she confided in her best friend.

"I think it's a sign," she told Lilly.

"Oh come on! You're just nervous. Getting married is a big step and of course you're scared. Don't worry, everything will be fine."

"But the dream, Lilly; I feel weird. Maybe I'm making a mistake."

"Marisha, think! You love Greg, you always have. Greg loves you, so why would it be a mistake to get married? Relax. One day we'll laugh about it, I promise." Lilly tried to reassure her.

"I don't know. I have this gut feeling that it's more than just nerves."

Marisha would have liked to believe that it was just a case of cold feet, but her unease grew stronger with each passing day. Her feelings towards Greg had changed as well. She wasn't as sure of her love for him as she had been before.

A week before the wedding, she'd noticed that she was seeing Greg in a completely different light and she didn't like what she saw.

How had she missed his mood-swings before? Why hadn't she noticed his bad temper? When did he start that annoying habit of grinding his teeth? On top of that, he'd bought a house and furniture and hadn't bothered asking her opinion. He was making major decisions that should involve them both. Why hadn't she questioned that before? Once she'd started, the questions and doubts kept flowing like a river.

But everything was set for the wedding and it was too late to back out. Marisha would have given anything to have someone to talk to. She couldn't talk to Greg, Lilly didn't take her seriously and Auntie Martha, well, that was gone too.

Shivers shook Marisha's body. That fatal week so many years ago was the beginning of the end for her.

The ringing phone brought her back to the here and now. She walked to the kitchen and picked up the receiver.

"Hello?"

"I'm sorry Marisha, I have to cancel tonight. Something's come up and I can't get out of it." Lilly's voice sounded strange.

"What is it? Are you okay?" Marisha was concerned.

"Yeah, everything is fine; I'll talk to you later."

"Lilly, you sound worried. Tell me what's wrong."

"Nothing. Must run. I'll see you tomorrow. Bye." Lilly hung up.

"Well, isn't that lovely?" Marisha thought. "I go out of my way to prepare a special meal for her and she cancels. Pay-back time, I guess."

Truth be told, Marisha was relieved that Lilly had cancelled their dinner date. She needed some time to herself to think things through.

Putting the roast into the freezer and turning the oven off, she filled a bowl with the freshly made salad and carried it into the living room. As she munched on the greens, she forced herself back to the wedding day.

She remembered making her way down the aisle. Nathan's firm grip on her arm kept her upright and moving forward. Her legs were shaking. Waves of nausea and panic attacked her body. Her aunt's "You'll never find true love!" echoed in her ears, but she walked forward. A steady stream of tears flowed from her eyes, but she walked forward. Every fibre of her being was screaming STOP! But she walked towards the man waiting at the altar.

Nathan lifted her veil, turned her to face Greg, then went back to stand beside Lilly.

One look at her husband-to-be and it became crystal clear that she was about to make the biggest mistake of her life. With fear gripping her heart and Aunt Martha's ugly words hammering in her head, Marisha gathered up the layers of her wedding gown and ran down the aisle towards the door.

Greg shouted her name, Lilly tried to block her way, but Marisha paid no mind. She ran out of the door, down the stairs, and kept on running until she had reached her apartment. She remembered the hours she spent face down on her bed. The wedding gown surrounded her like a white ocean. The tears that spilled from her eyes were hot tears of embarrassment. She knew that the look of astonishment and disbelief she'd seen in the faces of the friends and Greg's relatives gathered at the church that day would haunt her forever. The two pillows she threw over her head didn't block out the sound of fists pounding on her bedroom door.

"Open the door or I'll break it down! Now!" Greg was shouting nastily. Lilly and Nathan took turns pleading for her to let them in. Marisha didn't move.

The thunder of exploding wood ripped through the apartment. Greg stormed in, took hold of Marisha's arms and forced her off the bed. He slapped her across the face, calling her filthy names. His face was purple with rage. His nails were digging deeply into her flesh. Marisha felt no pain. She was numb. Greg raged on for an hour, demanding an explanation for her behaviour and why she'd embarrassed him in front of his family and friends. He was demanding answers, but didn't pause long enough to give her a chance to speak. Lilly tried to calm him down but he pushed her across the room. Nathan took a swing at him but he was no match for Greg. Marisha was totally at his mercy and Greg kept yelling and cursing and slapping until his anger was spent.

To this day, Marisha remembered his parting words: "You think you're too good for me? You should be kissing my feet, you bitch! You think you're something special, don't you? Well, I'm here to tell you you're nothing but a stupid, dumb Polack!" He threw her onto the floor and stormed out of the apartment. That was the last time Marisha saw or heard from him.

Until that day, she had never felt she was in a minority group. She was a landed immigrant and she had laughed along with her friends at "Did you hear about the dumb Polack who ..." jokes. That day changed her. She realized that she was carrying a label. Hearing Greg calling her "a dumb Polack" had placed her into a category.

From that day, every Polish joke offended her personally. She felt the full impact of the fun being poked at her country and she hated it. She was proud to be Polish. She'd made Canada her home but Greg had reminded her that she was a foreigner, an alien. Although she had lived in Canada longer than she had in Poland and her passport read "Canadian citizen," she was a stranger in this country. Greg's memorable parting words had disturbed her inner peace and left her restless and searching for a sense of belonging.

Marisha bit her lip. She felt uncomfortable thinking of that day and the days that followed. Everyone hated her. How could she explain to her friends that leaving Greg at the altar was justified only by her gut feeling? Even Lilly didn't fully understand and she had witnessed Greg's rage and abusive behaviour.

Although she had never regretted her decision, she felt bad for letting the wedding plans go that far. Nevertheless, she was glad that she'd had the courage to run. Yes, there were consequences. For the best part of that year, her friends wanted nothing to do with her. They all knew Greg and felt sorry for him. Movies, dancing and dating became things of the past. People pointed fingers at her and whispered behind her back.

A couple of times she had been asked out but when she went to the agreed place, her date was a no-show. She figured that someone had warned them about her. As far as she was concerned, she was cursed! The only person that stood by her side was Lilly. Dear, reliable Lilly.

Marisha's head hurt from the memories. She needed to escape the pain, even for a short time. She picked up her diary.

CHAPTER 7

DEAR DIARY,

Finally, I am in Canada. It has taken me almost two weeks to get over the plane ride. It was the longest trip ever!

By the time we landed in Canada, I felt like a robot. I didn't even have the energy to be scared or excited any more.

At the airport, I was met by three people—Auntie Martha, her husband Ted, and my dad's brother, Uncle Joseph. They all looked tired just like me. They all hugged me. I felt weird. They were all strangers, but they were very happy to see me. We went together to pick up my bag. Auntie Martha had told me how worried they were when the first plane came and I wasn't on it. They spent hours at the airport waiting for any news of my whereabouts. I felt so bad.

I'll never forget the trip from the airport. Uncle Joseph had brought his new car. The two men sat at the front and Auntie Martha and I sat in the back. Right from the beginning, I didn't like the smell of the car. We hadn't even left the airport parking lot before I had to get out. I prayed that I wouldn't get sick. I did! Before we got home, Uncle Joseph had to stop three times for me. My stomach hurt and I was throwing up all over Canada. Nice hey? I can't tell you how embarrassed I was.

By the time we got to the house, Uncle Ted practically had to carry me inside. I had no strength left, my face was green, and my whole body was shaking.

Auntie Martha made me some tea, and to tell you the truth, I don't remember drinking it.

I woke up early next morning, still on the sofa. God! I felt so ashamed. What did my new family think of me? My arrival sure wasn't the way I pictured it. I had gotten lost, threw up all the way home, and instead of visiting with my new family, I fell asleep! You can imagine how horrible I felt that morning.

Auntie Martha was the first to get up. She went to the kitchen and made breakfast. After we ate, I had a bath. Wow! I have never had a bath in such a big tub. The soap and the shampoo smelled so nice and the water was nice and warm. I felt like a princess. To have a bath back home, in Poland, we had to warm up the water on the stove, pour it into a metal tub, and wash. The tubs were too small to sit in.

I love Auntie Martha's house. It has three bedrooms up, and two more downstairs! It has a nice big kitchen and dining room. One big room Auntie Martha calls the living room, but I'm most amazed by the bathrooms. There are three of them in this house! I have never seen a house with its own bathroom inside, never mind three! The farms have

outdoor toilets. At Aunt Sonia's there were four toilets in the basement for
everyone in the building to share. This is heavenly.

I have my very own room, too. It has wallpaper with little pink
flowers, my bed with pink sheets and frilly pillows, and on top of all that,
I have new furniture. Everything is white, the dresser, the desk, and even
a little white chair. There are pink curtains in the window and beautiful
pictures on the walls. I have a closet for my clothes, shelves full of books
and, believe it or not, toys! Yes, toys.

I know what you're thinking—I'm too old for toys—but you should
see them. There are different sizes and colours of teddy bears, dolls dressed
in every possible fashion, puzzles and colouring books, and stuff I don't
even know. I have never dreamed of having such beautiful things.

Sometimes I think that none of this is real and that I'll wake up and
find myself back in Aunt Sonia's apartment. I even pinched myself once,
just to make sure. I'm so happy. Every day, I walk around with the biggest
smile on my face.

It is so nice to have someone care for me. I feel like a child. Auntie
Martha cooks and cleans. I try to help her but there really isn't much to
do. Her house is so clean. Actually, everything in Canada looks clean. A
couple of times we went for a walk around the neighbourhood and I was
surprised how nice and clean everything was. Even the streets are clean!
And the houses! Wow! I think everyone is very rich here. Would you believe
that every house has a grass patch in front? It's not a garden or anything,
just grass! Uncle Ted said that it was just to make the house look nice.
Imagine! If Aunt Sonia saw this, well, I know what she'd say—that it
was a waste of good soil.

I think everyone owns a car. Every house has a garage and there are
cars parked on the street.

Uncle Ted told me to sit in his car for a few minutes every day. He said that I have to get over the carsickness and get used to riding in a car as soon as possible. I'm trying. Uncle Ted's car doesn't smell as bad as Uncle Joseph's, maybe because it's not as new. I can sit in it with the door closed and I don't get sick. But when the car is moving, my stomach turns immediately.

Uncle Joseph suggested that next time I sit up front. He said sometimes that helps. Well, I'll try.

Last week we walked over to the shopping centre. What a treat that was! So many stores under one roof! I didn't know what to look at first. And the people! Everywhere I looked, people were buying something. I have noticed that the adults were dressed nicely but the kids looked grubby. Their clothes looked too big for them. I don't understand why. There were so many nice clothes in the stores, yet, all the teens wore almost rags. My first thought was that they bought bigger clothes so they can grow into them, but that didn't make sense. By the time they fitted, the outfits would be old. I asked Auntie Martha about that. She told me that was the fashion for teens. Strange, isn't it?

That day, Uncle Ted bought me a pair of jeans and new shoes. Auntie Martha helped me pick out a jacket. Boy! I was so happy. I'm glad I came to Canada.

I wear my jeans every day. It makes me feel American. The tennis shoes felt strange at first but now I love wearing them; they are very comfortable.

Uncle Joseph came to visit today. He has a house twenty kilometres from here, so he doesn't come often. He gave me fifty dollars. I didn't want to take it, but he said that it would make him feel good if he could buy me something. He's visiting with Auntie Martha and Uncle Ted now, so I came to my room to write.

I'm going to end this entry because my hand is getting sore and I still have to write a letter to Aunt Sonia. I have so much to tell her.

May 29th, 1975

Dear Diary,

Today, Auntie Martha and Uncle Ted went to a funeral. I didn't want to go with them. I don't like funerals.

A month has gone by and every day I thank the good Lord for bringing me to Canada. My life is a dream. I have a nice place to live, nice clothes to wear, and all the food I want to eat. I swear, if all the stores closed down, we could live a year on the food that's in this house. In Poland, we had to go shopping every day to buy food for lunch and supper. Auntie Martha shops once a week and she buys enough to last for days. Mind you, having a fridge, freezer and the cold storage room helps. We had no such things back home. Well, on the farms, we had root cellars, but they were just holes dug under the house and, other than potatoes, cabbage, and beets, you couldn't really keep anything in there.

At first, I had a problem getting used to the food. Everything tasted salty. But I'm over it now. I love oranges. Until I came here, I had never had an orange. Now I eat too many of them. I'm getting a rash. Uncle Ted said that it's from the acid in oranges.

In September, I'm going to start school. I don't know how I feel about that. Auntie Martha assures me that I'll love it. She says that I have to go to school, not only to learn English, but it is the law. You'd think that they'd ask me to go to work, wouldn't you? After all, I'm old enough to earn my keep. I have suggested that, but Uncle Ted just laughed. He said that I was too young to work and that I'd have plenty of time for work after I graduate. That blew me away. Imagine, at fifteen I'm too young to work! Heck! I've been earning money since I was ten!

My life here is unbelievable. All day long, I do whatever I want. Auntie Martha and Uncle Ted are so nice to me. Uncle Joseph comes every so often and takes me for an ice cream. Oh yeah, I forgot to tell you, I can ride in the car now. I have to sit up front and look straight ahead, but I don't get sick any more. Isn't that something?

July 18th, 1975

Dear Diary,

What a summer I'm having! Every day we go somewhere, so I don't even have time to write. Uncle Ted and Auntie Martha spend all their time with me. They took me to the library and the museum. We spent a day at the beach. The other day we went to visit their friends on a farm. Boy! The farm was nothing like the ones we have in Poland. I can't even begin to tell you how huge the farms are. And the equipment they use, well, let me just say I didn't know there were such machines. If Uncle Lech and Auntie Helen saw all this, I wonder what they'd say.

Last week, Uncle Joseph picked us up and we went fishing. I caught two fish, all by myself! I love fishing. We had a picnic and all.

Uncle Joseph told us that he had found a new girlfriend. Uncle Ted didn't think much of that. He said that Uncle Joseph has a talent for finding the craziest women. This is also new to me, Uncle Joseph having a girlfriend. I thought that only young boys had girlfriends. Uncle Joseph is forty-seven years old and he's not married. I wonder why? I would like to ask him, but I'm scared. It's none of my business, and it might offend him. Maybe, one day, I'll ask Auntie Martha.

On Sundays, we go to Polish church and afterwards we go to the restaurant for lunch. I always have French fries and orange pop.

Did I tell you that we have a colour television in our house? Every evening, after supper, Uncle Ted and Auntie Martha watch the news. I love looking at the TV, but I don't understand anything. Sometimes when there is a movie, Uncle Ted translates for me, but it's hard. They laugh at some shows and I just sit there and watch the pictures. When I go to school, I'll learn the language as quickly as I can, so I can watch TV and understand what's being said, too.

Aug. 16th, 1975

Dear Diary,

A letter from Aunt Sonia came today. She says that her health is poor, and with no family close by, she feels helpless. She has no one to go to the store, bring water, or run errands for her. Complaints, complaints, complaints. Not once did she say that she's happy for me. My letter to her was full of wonderful things I have seen in Canada. I told her about the house and my room. You'd think she'd be happy for me. But no! Same old thing—I'm sick, I'm dying, I have no one to look after me. It's not my fault that she has no husband or kids. When I was with her, it wasn't any better. She complained about everything all the time. As far as her health goes, I don't think she is sick at all. I think she's just looking for sympathy from everyone. Anyway, I'll take my time before I write back to her.

If I sound grumpy today, it's because I am. Something is bothering me. On Sunday, just before we went to church, I was combing my hair in the bathroom. The door was open and Uncle Ted came in. He came up behind me and put his hands on my shoulders. I looked at him in the mirror and smiled. He kissed the back of my head, and then, he slid his hand down the front of my blouse towards my . . . my . . . you know. I jumped and he took his hand back. He smiled at me but it wasn't his normal smile. It was somehow different.

I've been thinking about it for a long time and in the end I convinced myself that I imagined the whole thing. Uncle Ted was his normal, nice self. After church, we went to the restaurant and afterwards for a drive to visit Uncle Joseph. After a couple of days, I forgot about the incident.

Then something had happened again. Yesterday we were having breakfast. Auntie Martha got up to get some more toast and that's when Uncle Ted put his hand on my knee. I thought that he wanted to tell me something, you know, get my attention, but when I looked at him, he had that strange smile on his face. His hand was sliding up my thigh! I didn't know what to do. Thank goodness Auntie Martha came back. He put his hand on his own knee then.

I'm almost positive that if we had been alone, he would have slid his hand all the way up my dress! What am I to think about all this? He is such a nice man, so good to me, and I don't want any trouble. Can't talk to Auntie Martha about it, or can I? Geez! What should I do?

For now, I'll avoid being alone with him. With Auntie Martha around, Uncle Ted is nice and fun to be with.

Aug. 27th, 1975

Dear Diary,

For the past few days, I have been watching my aunt and uncle very closely. We're together all day long and we laugh a lot. Uncle Ted teases Auntie Martha as much as he teases me. As far as I can tell, they really love each other. When we go somewhere, they always hold hands, he kisses her quite often and they smile at each other a lot. Everything seems to be fine. So why is Uncle Ted coming after me like that?

Yeah, it had happened again. This time he kissed me right on the mouth. I was bringing a basket of raspberries from the garden. He stopped me in the entrance and told me that I had some raspberry juice on my face. When he took my chin in his hand, I thought that he was going to wipe the juice off. Instead, he wrapped his lips around my mouth.

Lord! That was so disgusting. His mouth was soft and wet, and he had bad breath. Yikes!!! Gagging, I pulled away just in time to catch a glimpse of Auntie Martha's face disappearing behind the living-room wall. He let me pass, and as if nothing had happened, he called to Auntie Martha, "Get ready—we're taking Marisha shopping for school supplies." Auntie Martha came into the kitchen, all smiles. I know she saw him kissing me, I'm sure she did!

Then he was back to normal. We went to the mall, he held Auntie Martha's hand, and he was nice to me. They bought me a load of school supplies, everything nice and colourful; you'd think that I'd be overjoyed. But I was too confused to enjoy myself. Why didn't Auntie Martha say anything? Do I talk to her about it? What am I supposed to do?

Oct. 21st, 1975

Dear Diary,

Sorry I don't write too often. To be honest, things are not going as well as they should. I'm in school all day and, surprisingly, I really like it. School is so different here. The teachers are nice and the students are friendly. My first two classes are Basic English. The language isn't as hard as I thought. The writing part is giving me problems. The spelling is the worst. But in time, it should all come together.

In my math class, there is this girl; her name is Lilly. She's very nice to me. I wish my English was better so I could talk to her. I think, eventually, we'll become friends. For now, we sit beside each other in class, we eat our lunches together, and we're trying to communicate without much success. Lilly is very patient and encouraging. She is very inventive too. Besides talking slowly and clearly, she carries a note pad so when everything else fails, she draws me a picture. I think I'm learning more from Lilly than from the teachers.

At home, things are not good at all. I'm afraid of Uncle Ted all the time. If Auntie Martha is not around, I hide or leave the house. I'm not kidding. He is like an octopus. He touches me every chance he gets. He tried to kiss me again, I pushed him away, and from that day, he's not very nice to me. He yells at me a lot and even calls me stupid when I don't understand something.

I tried to tell Auntie Martha about him touching me. Imagine my surprise when she told me that it was my fault. She said that I parade around in skimpy clothes and make goo-goo eyes at him, so I'm asking for it.

What does she mean by that? The clothes I wear, they chose and bought for me, and for the goo-goo eyes—I don't even know what that is!

It isn't much fun to be scared all the time. School is my safe place and I look forward to going there, but eventually I have to come back home.

Even the nights at home aren't safe. One time, I woke up in the middle of the night and he was there, in my bedroom, standing by my bed and looking at me! That freaked me out so badly! Now, before I go to sleep, I push the dresser against my bedroom door. I wish my door had a lock of some sort.

There goes my Polish luck again. I finally have a family to love, nice house to live in, my own room, and my happiness is spoiled by my uncle, Handy. That's my nick-name for him.

If Uncle Joseph ever gets married, maybe I could go and live with him. He has a girlfriend; she seems nice. Maybe, one day soon he'll marry her. I hope so.

Dec. 28th, 1975

Dear Diary,

School is out for Christmas break. This month wasn't too bad for me. Auntie Martha was getting everything ready for the holidays, so I was busy helping her. We baked, cleaned, and decorated the whole house with beautiful ornaments. Uncle Ted brought a huge Christmas tree and we spent a day hanging lights and ornaments on it. Everything looks so nice. Almost every house on our block is lit up with Christmas lights. In most windows, you can see the trees. The whole town looks magical.

I love going for a walk down the street, especially in the evenings. The lights from the houses and the trees throw colourful shadows on the newly fallen snow. Christmas music is playing and everything is so peaceful, so calm.

Sometimes, when I'm walking, I pretend that I'm going to my own home. My mom and dad are waiting for me. We have a nice house and a Christmas tree, and I'm just a normal teenager living with her parents in a safe, warm house, just like Lilly.

That girl is so lucky! I went to her house once. She invited me and two other girls from our math class to come for lunch at her place. Lilly's mom met us at the door and shook our hands. She talked to us and then she took us to the kitchen. It was hard for me not to cry, I was so envious of Lilly. Her mom was so nice. Her house felt so warm and comfortable. I can't describe the feeling that came over me that day. Lilly always complains about her younger brother. She says that he is a pest and that she hates him. Lord! What wouldn't I give to have her life, pest included! Trust me, I wouldn't complain about anything.

Wishing for something like that is just a fantasy. I know that. But I would be happy living with Auntie Martha, if only she hadn't married Uncle Ted, or maybe, if he had to go away somewhere far, far away. How about if he got sick and died, or got run over by a car or something. That's a horrible thought, I know, but I can't help it. I wish he was gone. He is so nasty to me sometimes.

Uncle Joseph came over for Christmas dinner. He brought his girlfriend with him. We had a nice time. We ate, talked, and opened presents afterwards. Auntie Martha and Uncle Ted bought me a new winter coat, jeans, and couple of sweaters. I love new clothes. Uncle Joseph bought me a small TV for my room. Wow! Isn't that something? My very own TV! But the best present was from Uncle Joseph's girlfriend. By the way, her name is Tina. Anyway, she gave me a box full of girl things. Make up, creams, shampoo, conditioner, and even some perfume. Just having those things in my room makes me feel like a lady.

Life would be so good if it wasn't for Uncle Ted. I hate fighting with him all the time. I hate him.

School will start again in January. I can't wait. I miss Lilly and I miss having somewhere to go every day.

Jan 9th, 1976

Dear Diary,

My prayers have been answered! Guess what? Uncle Ted is going away for two months! Yesterday, he received a letter from Poland. Apparently, his mother died and since he is her only child, it is up to him to deal with her estate. He's making the travel arrangements and I believe he'll be gone tomorrow or the next day. He wants to be there for the funeral.

I heard him tell Auntie Martha that he might have to stay in Poland longer than two months. His mother lived on their family farm with two of her cousins. Now that Uncle Ted is going to sell the farm, he feels obligated to find a place for the cousins. They ran the farm for many years, helping him and his mother, and he doesn't feel right about asking them to leave. Personally, I hope that it will take years for the land to sell, or maybe he'll lose his passport or something and won't be able to come back at all.

School is going well. My English is getting better every day. Lilly and I are good friends. We spend a lot of time together in school and on the phone. It's nice to have a friend.

Now for the sad news—Uncle Joseph broke up with Tina. Too bad. I was hoping those two would get married. What surprised me though is that he doesn't seem very upset about the break up. I think that I am more upset than he is. Oh well, maybe he'll marry the next one.

Feb. 25th, 1976

Dear Diary,

Time is going way too fast for my liking. A month has gone by since Uncle Ted left for Poland. Auntie Martha had a letter from him the other day. I guess he's decided to sign the land over to the cousins so they won't have to move. The paperwork is moving along and he thinks that he'll be coming back soon.

Every night I pray for some sort of delay. I don't want him back. I know that this sounds horrible but I even prayed for his plane to crash. I'm not proud of myself for having such mean thoughts, but how can I help it? Living with Auntie Martha, just the two of us, is like a dream come true. We've become really good friends. We go for walks, we play cards, watch TV, and walk around in the mall. I don't have to block my door at night and I feel happy.

Last weekend, Lilly came for a sleepover. That was one of the best weekends I have ever had. We had so much fun. Auntie Martha was very nice to Lilly and she even joined us in a game of rummy. Lilly and I slept downstairs. We talked halfway through the night, and slept until ten o'clock in the morning. Now I know how it would feel to have a sister. It would be a blast!

Lilly has invited me for a sleepover at her place next weekend. I didn't think Auntie Martha would let me, but after Lilly's mom talked to her, she said that it was okay. She even took me shopping for new pyjamas! She said that I had to look nice my first time away from home.

Yes, Auntie Martha is so much nicer without Uncle Ted around.

March 18th, 1976

Dear Diary,

He came back on March 15th. Auntie Martha was glad to see him and he seemed glad to see her too. I was the only one not happy at all. He hugged me and I felt his hands pinching my flesh. He had that look in his eyes, that dirty look.

All day, I did my best to stay away from him, but when I was washing up after dinner and Auntie Martha went downstairs to put a load of laundry in, he came up behind me and pressed himself against my back. His hands went to my breasts and he kissed my neck. Just then, Auntie Martha yelled out my name and ordered me to go to my room.

Humiliated and ashamed, I ran to my bedroom. After a good cry, I told myself that maybe it was a good thing that she saw us. Maybe now she'll tell him to stay away from me. God! I just wanted to die.

What happened next made me wish that I had never set foot in Canada. Auntie Martha came into my room and sat down on the chair. She stared at me for a long time and then she stood up and started yelling at me. She accused me of seducing her husband and called me a hussy, a tramp, and bunch of other nasty names. My mouth fell open. I couldn't believe that she saw all this as my fault! I wanted to defend myself, tell her that she had it all wrong, but what she said next stopped me cold. She said that I was a bitch sent from hell to ruin her happiness. That only the devil's spawn would wish for someone's death the way I wished for her husband's plane to crash. After he took me in, gave me a home, sent me to school, how could I wish death for him?

"Mark my words; scum like you never find true love. You'll be a lonely old spinster! God will punish you for this!" she threatened.

As she was yelling at me, the only thought going through my head was the fact that she had read my diary. I felt ill. My most private thoughts were written in this book and she'd read them.

It's not like I have left my diary lying around for her to see. From the first day, I hid it under the mattress or under my dresser. How could she?

Three days have passed. I go to school every morning, and prolong coming back for as long as I can. Neither Auntie Martha nor Uncle Ted speaks to me. It's very uncomfortable to say the least. I think they are wondering what to do with me. Maybe they'll send me back to Aunt Sonia's.

I found a new hiding place for my diary. In my closet, I lifted up a corner of the carpet and I'm sliding the book under it. You can't tell that it's there because the carpet slides back under the wooden casing.

March 26th, 1976

Dear Diary,

When I came home from school today, Uncle Ted followed me up to my bedroom but he didn't come in. He stood in the doorway and told me that he wanted to talk to me in the kitchen. I went to the kitchen, sat down at the table, and waited for the verdict.

To my surprise, he apologized for the mess he'd gotten me into and promised that he'd never touch me again unless I wanted him to. That's when Auntie Martha walked in. She stood in the doorway and stared at me, then at Uncle Ted. He told her that everything was fine, that I had admitted to him that I was wrong and that we wouldn't have any more problems.

What a liar! I hate him more than ever. How could he blame me for this? I hate Auntie Martha too because she believed him. All she said was "Good," and went back outside.

I was so angry, I started to cry. He patted my head. I pushed his hand away and ran out the door. I ran and ran until I reached the park.

March 12th, 1977

Dear Diary,

A lot has changed in the past year. I have a boyfriend now. His name is Greg. Lilly is dating Nathan. Lilly and I work as waitresses in the restaurant. After work, I spend time with Greg or with Lilly. I come home late at night, just to sleep, and usually I'm out before my aunt and uncle are up. I plan it that way. The less I see of them, the better. I have never forgiven Aunt Martha for snooping in my room and reading my diary. I don't trust her. That's the reason I stopped writing any more.

Uncle "Handy" tried to corner me a couple of times, but I'm not afraid of him any more. The first time he came at me, I screamed a blood-curdling scream and he backed off. The last and final time he tried to kiss me, I kneed him in the groin and told him that if he ever even looked at me the wrong way, I'd call the police. (Greg told me to say that. He also showed me the magic kick). After that, my uncle has not come near me. Too bad I didn't do all that sooner; maybe my life with them wouldn't be as bad.

Anyway, in six months, I'll be eighteen years old, and I won't have to live with them anymore. Greg and I will get married and we'll find our own place.

One good thing about avoiding my family is that I take every available shift at the restaurant. I work mega overtime and between the wages and the tips, my bank account is growing bigger than I'd ever hoped.

I haven't seen Uncle Joseph for a long time. A few months earlier, he came to my restaurant and told me that he was going to work up north somewhere.

I don't think I'll write any more. Good timing too, just one page left in this old book. If I change my mind and want to continue my diary, I'll get a real diary—one that comes with a lock and key.

For now, thank you for being good listener and for being my friend when I needed one the most. It was good to write when I had no one to talk to.

Now, I have Lilly and Greg and I think my life is turning around and my Polish luck is changing for the better.

Marisha Pawlak

CHAPTER 8

MARISHA CLOSED THE book and smiled a sad little smile. She had enjoyed reading it and regretted that it ended. She wished that she had written more. In a way, the Marisha who wrote this diary seemed like a different person—familiar, dear to the heart—but different from the Marisha holding the book now. When she was recording her feelings, everything was important, exciting and at times even tragic. Now, it was just a funny little story written by a teenager. If only the rest of her past could be just a funny little story. But Roman and Brian—they were real.

She met Roman a year after her "almost marriage" to Greg. He came to the restaurant for lunch and a week later asked her out. Starved for male companionship, Marisha gladly accepted his invitation to a movie.

It wasn't long before they fell in love. After dating for only seven months, they decided to get married. Once again, the wedding plans were put into motion. This time Marisha was involved in every detail. It was going to be a small wedding, just the family and a few of their closest friends. She wanted everything to be perfect.

Roman was gentle and fun to be with. Although he resembled Greg physically, his character couldn't have been more different. Where Greg was stubborn and bad tempered, Roman was easy going and gentle. With him, Marisha felt loved and protected.

There were no bad dreams or second thoughts to stop her this time. She couldn't wait to be Roman's wife. She even sent a wedding invitation to Auntie Martha and Uncle Ted.

When the day came, she arrived at the church fifteen minutes ahead of schedule. Lilly met her by the front door and told her that Roman wasn't there yet. She suggested that they should go upstairs for a little while. Reluctantly, Marisha followed her up the narrow staircase to a small room. The quietness inside was eerie and the girls found themselves whispering.

"Do you want anything to drink? I could go to the kitchen in the basement, and see if there is anything in the fridge," Lilly offered.

"No, I'm fine. I just want to get this part over and done with. The memories of my last trip to the altar have me scared out of my mind. Did you see my aunt and uncle? Are they here?"

"I don't know. When I went in, it was so dark in the church and I was half-blind from the sunshine outside. Besides, the place is packed," Lilly said.

Marisha remembered how anxious she felt that day. Something was bothering her, but she couldn't put her finger on it. She was worried that her relatives would cause trouble or that something else would go wrong, but she hoped that this time it was just her nerves. She had no doubt that marrying Roman was the right decision. Her half-panic was due to something else, pre-wedding nerves or something like that.

"I'll go and see if Roman is in. You stay here. I'll come and get you, OK?" Without waiting for her friend to reply, Lilly left the room.

Alone, Marisha let her eyes wander around the sombre little room. Everything was brown. Wooden furniture, the chairs, shelves, the floor, even the drapes—all different shades of brown. "I wonder what they use this place for. It's so depressing," she thought.

Failing to suppress the uneasy feeling, Marisha was glad to hear the approaching footsteps. Lilly came back with Nathan trailing close behind her. The look on their faces alarmed Marisha. She jumped to her feet.

"What's wrong?" she choked, fear gripping her throat.

"Nothing is wrong. Relax, will you? Roman is running late; the traffic must be bad," Nathan said with a conviction meant to reassure her.

"I knew it! I have this feeling that something isn't right, something has happened. Oh God! I knew I shouldn't have worn this dress! It's bad luck to wear the same wedding dress twice, especially if it didn't work the first time!" Marisha was aware that she was getting hysterical, but couldn't stop herself. Lilly took her by the hand and forced her to sit back down. In a calm but stern voice, she addressed her friend.

"Stop this nonsense! Your wedding dress is beautiful; it would have been a waste to spend money on another when you already had this one. Next month, I'll be wearing it to my wedding. If I thought for one moment that it was a bad luck, do you think I'd want to wear it? Roman is running late, no big deal, I'm sure he has a good explanation."

Dear, sweet Lilly. If only she'd listen.

Roman never did show up at church. One week later, his lifeless body was fished out of the lake. Homicide? Suicide? It was anyone's guess. No clues, no suspects, no Roman, and no wedding.

Marisha wanted to shred the dress, but Lilly insisted that she was going to wear it for her wedding. She didn't listen to Marisha's warning that there was a curse on that gown. Anyone else would have at least thought about it, but no, not Lilly! The ever—positive, look on the bright side, my cup is half-full Lilly had to find out the hard way. And she had, five months after her wedding. Not only did she lose her new husband, but the shock and grief also took her unborn child.

The day after the funeral, with wine and tears flowing freely, Lilly and Marisha held a wedding gown shredding and burning ritual.

CHAPTER 9

ON FRIDAY EVENING, Marisha answered the relentless ringing of her doorbell.

"Lilly!?"

Her friend was standing at the door, a large pizza in one hand and a bottle of wine in the other. Her eyes pierced Marisha.

"Yeah, it's me, Lilly. You do remember me?" Lilly's voice was laced with sarcasm.

"What . . . why . . . ?" Marisha stammered.

"This all ends now. You're going to talk to me whether you like it or not!" Lilly slid past her stunned friend. Marisha closed the door and followed her into the kitchen.

"You have been avoiding me for a week. If that's your punishment for my cancelling our dinner date, it's duly noted. But it has to stop right here, right now! Next weekend, we'll be stuck on the same plane and then in the same room for fourteen days; there will be no place to hide. So either we get things out in the open, and start being friends again or I'm cancelling my ticket. It's up to you. I was hoping that it wouldn't come to this, but you leave me no choice." Lilly set the pizza box on the table and went to the cupboard to get some plates. Marisha set out two wine glasses and worked on uncorking the wine bottle.

"I wish I could tell you what's wrong, but trust me, I can't," she said quietly.

"Try!" Lilly ordered.

Pouring the wine, Marisha considered her answer carefully. "My life is upside down. I think I'm going through a midlife crisis. That or maybe I'm going insane, you know, getting some sort of dementia," she confessed.

"Why do you think that?"

Plates loaded with pizza slices, wine glasses filled, the pair walked over to the living room. As they had done many times before, they settled on the floor with their backs resting against the sofa. From the time they were teenagers, this was their favourite position to watch movies, eat pizza, study, or just talk.

"Look at my life . . . how I screw up everything . . . it's not normal," Marisha said quietly.

"To be honest with you, two months ago, I was positive that you were demented. Twenty-two years you've waited for a guy like Brian to come along and when he did, what did you do? Why? Please tell me what the hell happened that day." Lilly studied Marisha's face over her slice of pizza. She knew that she came on strong, but if she gave Marisha half a chance, her friend would clam up and then how could she help her if she didn't know what the problem was? She had to get her talking. Marisha took a few bites in silence. She knew it was time to talk to Lilly, but she needed to form some sort of order before she answered.

"After Roman, I didn't think that I'd ever love again. As you said yourself, it took me over twenty years and a guy like Brian before I could consider a relationship." Pushing her plate away, Marisha fell silent. A nervous tic was jumping in her jaw line.

She took a long sip of wine, cleared her throat, but didn't say any more. Lilly noted the tic and the tears that were building up in Marisha's eyes. She gave her time to compose herself, then, in a soft voice, she asked again.

"So, what changed? Why didn't you go through with the wedding? You loved him, didn't you?"

"You know I did. It took a long time before I admitted it, even to myself. Still, when Brian asked me to marry him, I said no. I didn't want to . . . to . . . ." Marisha dropped her gaze to her hands. Lilly broke the momentary silence.

"Yes, I remember—the curse and all. But we've destroyed the dress. I thought that the curse was gone with it!"

"Well, so did I. That's why, eventually, I accepted Brian's proposal."

"But you didn't marry him! Why?"

"The curse, Lilly, the curse!"

"You've lost me. Marisha, you're not making any sense. Tell me what happened that day. We were all waiting at the church, you came in, but why did you quit halfway down the aisle? Obviously, you didn't think about the curse when you were getting ready. I was with you, remember? You seemed happy. You even told me "Number three was going to be the charm." Did your uncle say anything when he was walking you down the aisle?"

"Uncle Joseph? No. Oh God! I just remember how surprised he looked when I . . . when I stopped walking. Oh Lilly, I'll never forget the look on his face. But more so, the look of disappointment on Brian's face. Brian was devastated. When I left the church, I went to the hotel. I didn't want the history to repeat itself, you know, like what had happened with Greg."

"But why, Marisha, why did you walk out on Brian?" Lilly asked again.

"Oh Lilly, if I tell you, you'll have me committed! I think I'm going insane, really."

"Tell me what happened."

"Okay, but please . . . be open-minded."

"Marisha! For the love of God! Will you . . ." Lilly's temper flared up.

"OK, OK," Marisha cut her off. "After you left for the church, I went to my car. The windows were kind of' fogged up. Anyway, when I got in, I saw some writing on my windshield . . . and it freaked me out."

Marisha's voice trailed away. She looked as though she went into a hypnotic trance. Lilly wrapped her arms around her friend.

"I knew I should've insisted on driving you to your uncle's hotel that day. I shouldn't have listened to you."

"No . . . I wanted to be alone for few minutes, remember?"

"What was written on the windshield?" Lilly asked soothingly.

Marisha shifted uncomfortably and covered her face with her hands. She wasn't sure if she had actually seen the writing or whether her mind had played a trick on her.

"You can tell me," Lilly encouraged gently.

"Marry him and he'll die like Roman." Marisha's voice was no more than a whisper.

"What?" Lilly asked, confused.

"That's what was written on my windshield. Marry him, and he'll die like Roman."

"But . . . who? Why? I don't understand. Why didn't you tell anyone . . . Brian . . . or better yet, the police? At least me—you could have told me."

"The minute I drove into the sunshine, the sign was gone. I tried to tell myself that I had imagined the whole thing . . . blaming it on a case of cold feet. I couldn't tell anyone, because everyone was at the church, remember? How could I tell the police anything? The evidence was gone! It had disappeared! When I got to Uncle Joseph's hotel parking lot, I looked for any evidence of the message but there was nothing, absolutely nothing. Then, in Uncle Joseph's car, I convinced myself that I had imagined the whole thing. I was going to carry on as though nothing had happened, but I couldn't. I saw Brian waiting for me at the altar and I got scared. What if something happened to him . . . just because he had married me? How could I take a chance like that? That message—real or imagined—I believed it to be a sign. The curse lives on. I'm not meant to marry anyone. So by not marrying him, I let Brian live, you see?"

"Jesus Christ, Marisha, why didn't you explain all this to Brian. You owe him at least that much. Poor guy was going out of his mind! It was cruel not to give him any explanation."

"Lilly, think about my situation, do you think that anyone would have taken me seriously? They would have thought that I was nuts. Brian would have insisted that we went on with the wedding. I'd rather be alone for the rest of my life than have someone's death on my conscience. Tell me the truth; could you take a chance like that? Yeah, maybe the message meant nothing, but what if it did?" Marisha paused and waited to hear Lilly's answer.

"Why didn't you tell me?" Lilly asked.

"What would you say? You're crazy Marisha. You're just running scared, Marisha. Sorry Lilly, I couldn't take a chance on your talking me out of my decision."

"Fine, but why didn't you say something to me after . . . when the wedding was no longer an issue?" Lilly sounded hurt.

"I wanted to, but something else is going on. I tell you, my life has gone to hell. At work, I have someone watching me from the building across the street. At home, I'm getting phone calls from a heavy breather; I don't sleep at nights, and to tell you the truth, I'd be very surprised if I don't get the boot at work. My job has suffered as much as our friendship has. I don't want to drag you into this mess. What if I have some lunatic watching me, following me around? I don't want you to be caught in the middle. If anything should happen to you . . . well, I can't even think about it. You're all I've got left, Lilly." Marisha hugged her friend. "Please, don't be mad at me," she pleaded. Feeling a bit guilty, Lilly hugged her back. "I'm not mad at you . . . any more. I understand that you want to protect me, but who will protect you? I bet you didn't call the police about the stalker or the prank calls, did you? I won't let you go through this alone. We'll get to the bottom of it all, and we'll do it together, you and me, understood?" Marisha heaved a sigh of relief. It felt good to have Lilly's support. "I should have talked to her sooner," she thought with regret. Just talking about it and having it all in the open lessened her burden considerably.

"So, what will you do about Brian? He won't just go away, you know."

"He already has. I've told him that I never want to see him again. He didn't even ask why. He doesn't call me anymore."

CHAPTER 10

THEIR FLIGHT WAS scheduled for 5 a.m. Arriving at the airport at 4 a.m., both Marisha and Lilly were surprised to see the line-ups at the check-in counters.

"Holy cow! Looks like everyone is trying to get away from here," Lilly commented to her companion.

"Can you blame them? It's freezing outside. I can't wait to step outside into the sunshine and tropical warmth," Marisha replied with a smile.

Half an hour later, passing through the security gate, Marisha caught her breath.

"Look, there is . . ."

"Who?" Lilly tried to follow her friend's line of vision.

"Oh . . . nobody. I thought that guy looked familiar."

"What guy?" Lilly wasn't giving up.

"Never mind, it was nothing." Marisha wanted to drop the subject. Truth be told, she had a feeling that someone was watching her. When she'd turned her head, across the crowd, she caught a glimpse of a man staring at her. His face looked familiar, but she couldn't think where she'd seen him before. Before she had a chance to take a closer look, the man had disappeared into thin air. Cold shivers ran through her body and she fought hard not to show the panic that was building up inside her. It wouldn't do any good if both she and Lilly started their trip with the suspicion and paranoia of being followed and spied on.

Later, sitting on the plane, Lilly started a conversation with a young couple occupying the seats across the aisle. Marisha used that time to check out the male passengers sitting in the rows ahead. None of them looked familiar. Craning her neck, she looked to the back. A couple of rows behind, she met two pairs of male eyes staring directly at her. One man looked away, but the other held her gaze. She spun forward. Neither of the men looked familiar yet something about them bothered her. The pair made an odd couple. They didn't look like tourists, they didn't look like business men, they looked more like a couple of spies from some low budget movie. That thought made her chuckle. "I'm being paranoid. Now I think that everyone is after me. Gosh! I have to pull myself together."

Afraid that Lilly might notice her unease, Marisha was grateful for the in-flight movie. The flick was interesting and they spent an hour and a half watching it in total silence. At times, she even managed to forget her earlier suspicions.

Deplaning, Marisha secretly watched for the face she'd seen at the other airport. To her relief, the only faces she recognized belonged to the odd couple, the spies. Although they walked to the same baggage carousel and later boarded the same tour bus as Lilly and Marisha, they paid no attention to either of the girls. Marisha allowed herself to relax and suppress her overactive imagination.

The tour guide welcomed everyone to Mexico and informed them that their destination resort was about an hour away. Along the way, he talked about the history of different points of interest and proudly pointed out prestigious golf courses and some houses owned by famous people.

The outskirts of Cabo San Lucas had a different effect on the girls. Lilly commented how poor the city looked. The ongoing construction had left the roads and sidewalks in a state of mess and chaos. Houses were covered with dust and above all everything looked poor. The only greenery seemed to be around the resorts and the gulf courses.

Marisha could see past the dust and the construction. She was in awe of the blue, sunny sky, the palm trees standing tall and majestic. The aqua greens and blues of the nearby ocean held her mesmerized. Her heart went out to the construction workers labouring in the heat and the groundskeepers grooming the lawns and she gave them credit for making their city a better, nicer place.

All of a sudden, Lilly was nervous about the resort where they would stay.

"What if the place is a dump?" She voiced her concern.

"Relax. They wouldn't call it a four-star resort if it was a dump. Besides, we've seen the brochures. The Palace looks nice," Marisha reassured her.

The bus turned off the main street and started an easy but steady climb through the side streets. Rows of small houses lined both sides for the first part but soon they were driving under an archway and down a winding driveway lined with palm trees and flowering shrubs.

"Oh my Lord! It can't be . . . Do you see what I see?" Lilly was squealing with joy.

In the distance, they could see the red roofs and snow-white walls of the Tropical Palace. It looked massive, to say the least. Three stories high, it spread wide and deep into the tropical landscape. As the bus neared the lobby entrance, everyone on board applauded.

Stepping out into the sunshine, reluctantly, people made their way inside. They were greeted by a hostess and led into an open-air room. Tables were set with tropical drinks of different varieties, trays of fruit and several trays of cold cuts and cheeses. Mexican music was playing softly in the background. Birds were chirping, and the chatter of the guests somewhere below set the holiday mood. Marisha and Lilly helped themselves to a drink and, with the rest of the new arrivals, stood and listened to their hostess's instructions concerning their luggage, rooms and the facilities the resort had to offer.

Since it was going to take some time to get into their room, Marisha and Lilly picked out a table near the railing and sat there admiring the view. Although the front of the lobby was a ground-level entry, the back of it hung three stories high. With no walls, front or back, one could see the breath-taking view right through the building. From their front-row seating on the third floor, Marisha and Lilly had a bird's eye view of the grounds, the beach and the ocean.

Directly below, another terrace was set with tables and chairs and had a small, open-air bar at the end. One floor lower was yet another terrace and another room with a roof and no walls. The Palace grounds were split into two halves, each being a mirror image of the other. Identical landscape, walkways, swimming pools, swim-up bars, cabanas, even the lounge chairs were set in the same pattern. Colourful hedges, manicured to perfection, rosebushes and flowering shrubs lined the walkways and pathways, dividing the areas for sun-worshippers' privacy. The red, pink and magenta flowers stood out brightly against the white cement, blue water, and the greens of the leaves. Green umbrellas and palm trees completed the picturesque grounds.

"This place is heavenly! Look at the beach. White sand for miles and miles—and the ocean! I think I've died and gone to heaven!" Lilly couldn't hide her enthusiasm.

Marisha took the opportunity to tease her. "So you're telling me that you won't mind spending the next two weeks in this dump after all?"

"Oh, shut up! I was worried for a bit, that's all." Lilly pulled a face.

The hostess came back and announced that the rooms were ready. One by one, she called out the guests' last names and handed out small white envelopes containing room keys. She also assured them that everyone's luggage was already in their rooms. Marisha's and Lilly's room was on the second floor.

Walking down the long, tiled corridors in silence, the friends took in the beauty of the Palace. They agreed that whoever had designed this building had done a splendid job. The décor was unique and truly worthy of a palace. The arched hallways, the statues, paintings and the floor tile design perfectly suited the place and its name. On one side of the hallways were archways with black wrought-iron railings instead of walls and windows. On the other side, spaced out evenly, were short hallways leading to two rooms with their doors facing one another. Spotting the number corresponding with the one on the envelope, Marisha swiped the key card and opened the door.

"This is unbelievable!" Lilly looked around the room with child-like excitement. "I have never stayed at a fancy place like this. Look, we even have our own bar! We're having a shot of tequila, right now!" Lilly picked out two shot-glasses and filled them with an amber liquid. Then she saw the fridge. Opening the door, she whistled, "Get a load of this! We have beer, juice, water, and fruit!"

Listening to Lily's chatter, Marisha walked around and admired the room. High ceilings, white stucco walls, and the heavy, dark mahogany woodwork and furniture were perfectly accented with colourful drapes, pillows and artwork. In their sunken sitting room, a huge patio door led to a good-sized balcony. Marisha stepped outside and drew a deep breath of tropical air.

"Nice, hmm?" Lilly handed her a shot-glass with tequila and a bottle of beer.

"It doesn't get better than this. We have an ocean in front of us, paradise, park-like grounds under our nose, and miles of white sandy beach in between. And look over there," Marisha pointed to the island. "Do you know what that is?"

"Isn't that Cabo San Lucas landmark . . . the lovers' rock, or lovers' beach or something like that? You know, the one with the arch resembling a drinking dinosaur?"

"Yeah-ha. And look at the cruise ships around there—people come from all over to look and take pictures. You and me, for the next two weeks, we'll be looking at it from our balcony, every day. Not bad for a view!" Marisha lifted her shot-glass in a salute, tossed her head backwards and downed the tequila in one gulp.

"Bravo!" Lilly followed suit.

"Hey, let's unpack, put our shorts on, and then we'll come out here to have our beer," Marisha suggested.

"Sounds good to me," Lilly agreed.

A few hours later, Marisha and Lilly left their room in pursuit of a restaurant. It was nearing five o'clock and they were reminded that the light lunch served on the plane was the only meal they'd had all day.

The brochures in the room mapped out all the places one could eat. Most of the restaurants required a twenty-four hour reservation, but the main restaurant was open for dinner from 4 p.m. until 9 p.m., and reservations were not necessary. They decided that, starting tomorrow, they'd eat at a different place every day. That was the beauty of going all-inclusive; you could try everything.

Tonight, they just wanted to eat, go back to the room, spend an hour or so relaxing on their balcony, and go to bed at a decent hour. The trip to Mexico wasn't long, but they had been up at 3 a.m. and with the change of climate, consumption of tequila and the beer, and no food to speak of, their energy levels were running low.

The restaurant they entered was huge. It had very high ceilings trimmed with red mahogany and there must have been at least a hundred tables. Each table was covered with a white tablecloth and decorated with placemats, colourful runners and flower arrangements. Self-serve buffets loaded with salads, fruit, desserts and numerous other delicacies cut the room in half and stretched the length of the restaurant. Against the walls, cooking stations offered a variety of freshly cooked meals.

Lilly had insisted that she would try everything but with such a variety, she had to admit that it was impossible to do it in one meal.

The minute they brought their plates to the table, the waiter appeared offering a choice of wines or any other drink. The food was delicious, the service excellent, and they couldn't have asked for a nicer atmosphere.

The young couple from the plane stopped by to say hello and exchange pleasantries. At the same time, Marisha noticed the "spies" sitting a few tables over. After the couple left, she pointed out the spies to Lilly.

"You're right, they do look like spies." Both girls giggled.

"The tall one is sort of cute. Maybe we can hang out with them later, you know, drinking, dancing, whatever." Lilly was eyeing the two men with interest.

"Lilly, cool your jets. Maybe they don't want to hang out with us."

"Do you think they're gay?"

"I don't know . . . maybe. Don't you find it odd that two men came to a resort . . . for a holiday . . . together?"

"Didn't you see the plumbers' convention from Calgary? There must be eight or ten of them. They came to the resort together," Lilly reasoned.

"Well, that's different. There are few of them; they're here to party. Don't get me wrong, the spies might be here just like you and me, I'm just not used to seeing two men holidaying at a resort unless they are a couple. Two guys travel together for fishing or a hunting trip, maybe skiing, but to a resort? Come on!" Marisha was sceptical.

"Well, tomorrow we'll check the place out. I wonder if there are some singles here. You'd think that mostly couples would come to a place like this."

"It doesn't matter, we came here to relax, suntan, and enjoy fourteen wonderful days of freedom. We don't need men to have fun," Marisha said.

"True. But it would be fun to have someone to dance with."

"I'll dance with you," Marisha offered jokingly.

Lilly laughed. "I just got the visual on that . . . lights are dimmed . . . romantic music playing . . . couples dancing and kissing . . . and there is you and me, dancing together . . ."

Marisha had to stop her. "Okay, so it's not the same, but we can rock-and-roll without looking silly, can't we?"

Chatting and laughing, the women finished their dinner and walked slowly back to their room. They were surprised to see the spies entering the room across from theirs.

Lilly thought nothing of it, but Marisha found herself thinking that maybe it wasn't a coincidence: "What if they are following us? But why? What for?"

She didn't share her concerns with Lilly. "No use getting her all worked up. Most likely I'm overreacting as usual," Marisha thought before she fell asleep.

CHAPTER 11

AFTER A DAY of sun tanning, swimming and relaxing by the pool, Marisha and Lilly were getting ready for dinner. Since they had forgotten to make reservations elsewhere, they had no choice but to eat at the main restaurant again. It wasn't a big deal though; they had plenty of time to try out the other places. And with the variety of dishes served at the main restaurant, they could eat there ten times and still wouldn't have to eat the same thing twice.

"Wow! Look at this, I have a tan already." Lilly was checking her arms.

"I can't wait to be brown like the rest of the people here. Did you notice how fluorescent the new arrivals looked at the beach? Sure easy to tell who just got here," Marisha said, spreading lotion on her legs. Lilly nodded in agreement. "What are we doing after dinner?" she asked.

"How about we walk around and see what they've got here."

The restaurant was buzzing with people. While Lilly was stuffing her face with food, Marisha was admiring the décor of the buffet. There were several melons carved to resemble birds and animals, and a few varieties of smaller melons cut in the shapes of tropical flowers, all tucked between salads, fruit and vegetable trays, creating a very colourful, artistic display.

"What are you looking at?" Lilly wanted to know.

"The pineapple palm trees on the buffet, aren't they cute?"

"Yeah, I love this whole place. Hey, check out the spies. The tall one looks pretty good in shorts. Don't look now, but they're staring at us," Lilly whispered.

The two men from the plane were making their way down the salad bar. Once they had passed their table, Marisha whispered back to Lilly, "I still say there is something strange about those two."

After dinner, they went to the reservation desk and booked a table for the next day at a Mexican restaurant. Then they strolled around the resort. Checking out the spa, hair salon and a couple of trinket stores, they ended their tour on the second-floor terrace.

This was the heart of the resort, the main entertainment area. The large, tiled floor was set with little tables. A stage took up most of one wall. There was a good-sized dance floor in front of it. Half of the room was under the roof and the other half was in the open. The open side had a small bar tucked away in the corner and the other much bigger bar was under the roofed part.

The place was almost empty. The nightly entertainment wasn't due to start for another hour and the small bar was closed, so Lilly suggested they order a drink at the bigger bar, relax and wait for the show to start. There were only two couples occupying the stools around the bar and one of the couples was the spies, as Lilly and Marisha had named them. Marisha was hesitant, but Lilly's mind was set and she wouldn't take no for an answer. She headed for the bar and somewhat reluctantly, Marisha followed.

The large oval-shaped bar was made of red mahogany with a marble counter top. Four mahogany pillars supported a massive canopy, which held dozens of glasses of different sizes. With bright lights, colourful bottles and several comfortable-looking mahogany stools, the bar looked inviting. Two very friendly young bartenders welcomed Lilly and Marisha and took their orders. Another couple took seats at the bar. The husband was well into the happy hour already and he figured that everyone was his friend. Making his rounds through the bar, he introduced himself as Alex. His wife, Rhoda, apologized for her husband's behaviour, but it was obvious that she wasn't upset by it. She laughed at him and joked with the people he approached. Alex insisted that everyone at the bar introduce themselves and say where they were from. Before long, everyone was involved in a general conversation.

Three more men joined the group. They were in their forties and, listening to their accent, Marisha guessed that they were from Texas. The group kept the bartenders so busy that they had to call for re-enforcements. A pretty Mexican girl was sent to the rescue. But when the plumbers' convention joined the party, even three bartenders couldn't keep up. Being the only single women in the group, Marisha and Lilly quickly became the centre of attention. With rounds of drinks and shooters, the laughter and conversations around the bar, no one had paid much attention when the stage curtain went up and the entertainment started.

One of the Texans had singled out Lilly and they were making plans to meet at the disco after the show. It wasn't like a date, it was just agreed that everyone would go there at the same time. Noticing that her glass was empty, Marisha spun her stool around to face the bar, and without much success, tried to get a bartender's attention. All three bartenders were busy at the far end of the bar, but right in front of her, she saw the top of someone's head. Hoping to get his attention, she patted her hand on the counter.

"Excuse me; I would like another gin, please."

The head bobbed up above the counter and Marisha was looking into the black eyes of a handsome Spaniard. Unable to look away, she had to tilt her head up when the bartender stood up. Marisha's gaze slid down to his mouth. Like his co-workers, he had a wide, friendly smile, and his parted lips had revealed two rows of perfect, snow-white teeth. His handsome, tanned face was framed with jet-black hair and eyebrows, giving a strong contrast to the crisp, white collar of his shirt. His eyes were focused on Marisha, but she was positive that he either hadn't heard her order or didn't speak a word of English. She cleared her throat and tried again.

"I . . . I . . ."

Her mouth refused to form the words. Moistening her dry lips with the tip of her tongue, she noticed that the tip of the Spaniard's tongue was slowly working its way along his top teeth. His absent-minded act wreaked havoc with Marisha's emotions. His eyes were fixed on her mouth. She caught her breath. "God! He doesn't even know he's doing that," she thought. When his eyes met hers again, she felt her cheeks flaming, but wasn't able to break the eye contact.

"You . . . wa . . . ?" The bartender uttered the two syllables and then just stood there, openly staring at Marisha. Marisha was staring back. All the background noise faded and her mind was absent of a single thought.

"Gin and tonic, easy on the ice." Lilly's voice startled both Marisha and the bartender. Lilly looked from one to the other and a wide smile spread across her face. Looking at the bartender's nametag, she clapped her hands. "Drake, is it? Come on, chop-chop! My friend is dying of thirst over here," she joked.

A friendly smile still on his face, Drake busied himself with the drink.

Marisha felt as though she was waking up from some strange dream. Momentarily confused, she looked at Lilly as though surprised to see her. Her friend smiled a knowing smile and turned her attention back to the Texans.

Drake put a drink in front of Marisha.

"Senorita," he said, and gestured towards the glass.

She wanted to say "Gracias," but the word flew out of her head. She wanted to say "Thank you," but didn't have any more success with that. One of the other bartenders, Eduardo, came up and whispered something to which Drake nodded and, with a smile in Marisha's direction, followed Eduardo to the end of the counter.

Marisha picked up her drink and exhaled. She wasn't aware that she had been holding her breath. "What the heck happened? Oh my God!" She pushed her glass away. "No more alcohol for me!"

Lilly had noticed her friend's manoeuvre and pushed the drink back towards her.

"Oh no you don't! We are getting hammered tonight! Come on, girlfriend, don't you dare chicken out on me," she warned. A couple of the plumbers, all three Texans, and even the tall spy joined Lilly in coaxing Marisha to have a drink. She had no choice but to join her friend in partying. But every chance she had, she'd secretly glance at Drake. Once or twice, their eyes met and she turned away guiltily. Each time he was serving someone across from her, she'd watch his back until he made a move to turn around, then she'd quickly look away. She noted that compared with Eduardo and the other bartender, Drake was a giant. He stood six-foot-something, a good foot above his co-workers. "Maybe he isn't Spanish. He looks Spanish though. I wonder if he speaks English. When people order drinks, he just smiles and mixes. Why doesn't he talk, like Eduardo? That one is a regular chatter box." She was trying to figure it out.

Realizing that Max, the tall spy, was talking to her, Marisha abandoned her preoccupation with the bartender and tuned in.

"And you haven't heard a word I've said, have you?"

"Sorry Max, it must be the tequila bangers. I find myself drifting off to la-la land. I'm not used to drinking that much, I guess." She hoped that her excuse was convincing. She couldn't tell the truth. What would she say? "Sorry, but I'm having a mid-life crisis, or maybe a breakdown. See that handsome bartender? I want to go up to him, and mess up his perfectly gelled hair and that's not all I want to do to him." No, she couldn't say that.

To her relief, Max bought the tequila story.

A round of applause stopped all the conversations around the bar. The entertainers finished their last set and the audience was showing their appreciation. Guiltily, Marisha joined in the applause. In truth, she hadn't heard or seen a single set.

Reaching out to pick up her glass and not finding it where she'd left it, Marisha turned her stool to face the bar and her blue eyes were met, square on, by those of the Spaniard. He was holding her almost empty glass and with a gesture of his hands was silently asking if she wished another. Marisha opened her mouth to say yes, but no sound came out. She nodded her head instead. Smiling and nodding back, Drake walked away to the mixing station. She watched his every move as he fixed her gin and tonic. Setting it in front of her, he said the only word she'd heard him say all night.

"Senorita."

Once again, Marisha wondered if he spoke English.

The group around the bar had almost doubled in size. Marisha looked around for Lilly. Her friend was surrounded by men and she looked as though she was having fun. Some fellows from Las Vegas came up to stand with Marisha, Max and the plumbers. The newcomers introduced themselves as Rob and Adam. It was obvious that Adam was an entertainer wherever he went. He was telling jokes and funny stories, bugging his friend mercilessly and hitting shamelessly on every female in range, Marisha included.

When the music from the adjoining disco reached their ears, everyone staggered towards the open doors. Within minutes, the dance floor was crowded. Dancing to almost every song, Marisha couldn't remember ever having so much fun. She'd even managed to put Drake out of her thoughts until much later when they were walking back to their room. With the two spy escorts, they passed the now empty bar and Marisha felt the same rush.

Later, in the privacy of their room, Lilly and Marisha compared notes from the evening. The alcohol kept them giggling until Lilly passed out cold. Marisha tried to analyze the Drake situation, but she didn't get past his almost black eyes before she had joined her friend in slumber.

CHAPTER 12

THEY COULDN'T HAVE asked for better weather. Sunshine, a clear sky and a gentle breeze coming off the ocean made their time at the beach a very pleasant one. However, a short walk down to the water's edge and a swim in the ocean left Lilly scrambling for her blanket.

"Man! I'm never drinking again! My head feels like it's going to explode," she complained, looking to her friend for sympathy. Plopping herself on a blanket next to Lilly's, Marisha chuckled.

"Serves you right! But the hangover aside, we did have fun last night, didn't we?"

Actually, Marisha was surprised that she didn't feel as sick as Lilly did. As far as she remembered, she had drunk as much as Lilly. The only difference was, other than the shooters, Marisha had stuck with gin and tonic, where Lilly was ordering a different drink every couple of rounds. Marisha speculated that Lilly's hangover was most likely caused by mixing drinks.

"Gosh, yeah! Last night I danced more than I have in my entire life, put together," Lilly exaggerated. "But hey, tell me, what was that staring contest you were having with Dracula?"

"Dracula?" Marisha burst out laughing. "Why on earth do you call him Dracula?"

"Oh, I don't know . . . maybe because he looks like one?" Lilly teased.

"Yeah, you're right, with his black hair all slicked back and his extra-white teeth. He does look as though he's from Transylvania," Marisha agreed laughingly.

"So, do you like him?"

"There is something about him that drives me crazy. I can't even talk normally when he's looking at me, and yeah, I like him," Marisha admitted shyly.

"That's good. I'm glad for you. Who knows, maybe you'll have a holiday romance? Wouldn't that be an adventure?"

"Wow! Slow down. I like the way he looks, but romance? Come on! I'm pretty sure he doesn't even speak English," Marisha protested.

Lazing in the sun, they talked about all the people they met the night before, the fun they'd had at the disco and how lucky they were to be away from their jobs.

On the way to their room, Marisha noticed that the spies were also making their way down the long hallway. She hadn't seen them earlier and wondered where they were coming from. It seemed that wherever she and Lilly went, they were close by.

Later, while enjoying Mexican cuisine, Marisha was surprised to see the spies again, just a few tables over.

"Do you think they're following us?" she asked Lilly.

"Why would you ask that? What possible reason would they have to follow us? We're all in the same building; of course we'll run into them everywhere," Lilly reasoned.

"I don't know. It's just weird that every time I turn around, they're there, behind us, in front of us, it's weird," Marisha said.

During dessert, Lilly broke the momentary silence.

"Great, now you have me paranoid. I could swear that that man, over there," she pointed in the direction of the beach, "has just looked at us through his binoculars."

Marisha strained her eyes. "That's him! The guy from the airport! I'm pretty sure I know him from somewhere."

"You know, he does look familiar," Lilly agreed. Craning her neck, she looked up and down the beach. "Where did he go?"

The man had disappeared, just as he did at the airport. Marisha stood up to get a better view. "Unbelievable, he's gone!" she exclaimed with a look of astonishment.

"Did you see him on the plane?" Lilly asked.

"I looked for him, but I didn't see him," Marisha admitted.

"Oh well, we're bound to run into him sooner or later. Funny though, we both think he looks familiar, yet we don't know who he is."

"Did he really look at us through binoculars?" Marisha enquired.

"It looked that way to me," Lilly answered.

"I was positive that he was spying on us at the airport, too. I saw him looking straight at me and when I looked, he disappeared, just like now." Marisha shivered. "Creepy."

"Okay, that's enough. Let's forget the creep or he'll ruin our fun. It's probably our imagination working overtime and if we're not careful, we'll think that everyone is out to get us—the spies, the creep, the Texans—maybe even Dracula." Lilly tried to lighten the mood and she succeeded. Marisha joined her in hearty laughter. Nevertheless, walking back from the Mexican restaurant, both Lilly and Marisha periodically looked over their shoulder, just in case.

As they came towards the main terrace, the mahogany bar stood out like a beacon. From afar, Marisha's eyes picked out Drake. He had his back to her but with his head towering above Eduardo, there was no mistaking him for anyone else. Approaching the bar, she noticed that Drake was talking to a customer. Hoping to hear the language they were using, Marisha slid silently onto a stool. Lilly, however, dragged her stool a good foot before she sat down. Hearing the stool being moved, Drake stopped talking, turned his headed and headed in their direction.

"Hola. Como esta?" Drake reached for Lilly's hand.

"Muy bien, gracias," she replied easily.

Drake moved in front of Marisha and repeated the greeting. Marisha was familiar with Spanish pleasantries, but the minute her hand landed in Drake's, every word escaped her memory, English included!

Drake lifted her hand and keeping eye contact, brushed his lips over her fingers. Mesmerized by his dark eyes, Marisha caught her breath. Slowly, a big smile spread over the bartender's handsome face. Reluctantly, he released her hand and turned to Lilly.

"Una Cerveza, por favor," Lilly ordered.

"Si." He faced Marisha, "Senorita?"

One simple word, and yet Marisha had no idea how to reply. She knew that he was waiting for her to order a drink, but for the life of her she couldn't utter a single syllable.

"She'll have a gin and tonic, easy on the ice," Lilly came to the rescue.

Watching Drake walk to the other side of the bar, Lilly smacked Marisha on the arm.

"What the hell is wrong with you? You look like a love-struck teenager!"

"God! I hate myself! I don't know what's happening to me. I feel like an idiot when he's looking at me," Marisha confessed.

"The way he looks at you, I think he likes you too ..."

Their conversation was interrupted by the boys from Texas. Coming back from parasailing, they stopped to visit with the girls. Lilly wanted to know every detail of their experience. She wanted to try parasailing herself, but neither she nor Marisha were sure if they'd work up enough courage to actually do it.

Drake placed a beer in front of Lilly, and placing a glass of gin in front of Marisha, he opened his mouth to say something. To Marisha's disappointment, one of the Texans called out.

"Senor Drake, we need some drinks here, por favor."

Drake's smile faded for an instant, but the minute he faced his other customers, the pearly-whites were in business again. From beneath her lashes, Marisha watched Drake as he listened to the orders. "What is it about this man that makes me so tongue-tied?" she thought.

She was hoping to hear him speak, but he had only smiled and nodded his head. His was the most amazing smile Marisha had ever seen. Most people smiled with their mouth only, but Drake's whole face lit up and his smile reflected in his eyes. Studying his smile, she hadn't noticed that Drake was openly staring back at her. Lifting her eyes to meet his, she felt her cheeks flaming. The bartender winked and with a chuckle turned back to his task.

Embarrassed, Marisha was cursing herself under her breath; then she heard Lilly's voice.

"Hey, Drake, what time do you work till?"

"Midnight." He had a Mexican accent.

"Why don't you join the rest of us at the disco, after?"

From the expression on his face, it was difficult to tell if he liked, hated, or simply didn't understand what Lilly had asked him. His black eyebrows went up, one corner of his mouth shot up, and he raked his fingers through his hair. "Gracias," was the only word he said before he followed Eduardo out the side door. Marisha wanted to pinch Lilly for putting him on the spot like that.

"What are you doing? You've embarrassed him, not to mention me! Jesus, Lilly! I'm not going to disco. I want to crawl under the carpet."

"Relax. He doesn't know I've invited him for you. I asked him, remember? Besides, I can see you want him and if you weren't such a chicken, you'd ask him yourself."

"Oh, I hate this. I'm going back to the room. You do what you want." Marisha attempted to stand up but Lilly held her arm.

"Stop it! You're acting like a kid. We're going to have fun tonight. Dracula probably won't even show up. Didn't you get the feeling that he hasn't understood a word I said to him? Look, I'm sorry if I made you feel uncomfortable, but really . . . we're here to have fun so don't worry, be happy. OK?"

If Marisha was going to protest any further, she wasn't given a chance. Loud applause broke out through the room as the entertainers spilled out onto the stage. Tonight's performance was the "Grease" musical, and the black leather jackets and poodle skirts twirled to the fifties tunes, making any conversation impossible. Alex came to the group, and invited everyone to join him and Rhoda at the table. He said that they'd managed to pull few tables together and there was plenty of room for everyone. Marisha was grateful that she could escape before Drake returned. Eduardo was back behind the bar but, as of yet, there was no sign of Dracula.

It wasn't until an hour or so later, when Marisha glanced in the direction of the bar that her eyes were met by those of the bartender. An involuntary smile lit up her face. She quickly looked away but his eyes were on her, she could feel it. Stealing a glance over the rim of her glass confirmed her suspicion—he was looking at her. "Why does it feel like he can see my very soul? Like he can read every thought I think, and he knows what kind of person I am? I don't know anything about him, and yet I feel as though I've known him all my life." Shivers ran down her spine. "I must be losing my mind. First the stalker, then the spies, and now this! Lord, I need to put all this out of my mind. I came here to relax, to forget, and not to drive myself insane."

Although Marisha had never been one to indulge in alcohol, she had decided that tonight she'd join Lilly and the others in a carefree evening of drinking and dancing. Tomorrow, she'd suffer the consequences and maybe the pain of a good hangover would dull her overactive imagination.

By the time they made their way to the disco, Marisha was well on her way to being intoxicated. She was giggling at anything and when on her way to the washroom she came face to face with the man from the airport, all she could do was burst out laughing. The man gave her a disgusted look and retreated into the men's room.

"You shouldn't be wandering around here alone. Where is your friend Lilly?" Max the spy took hold of Marisha's arm and gently but firmly escorted her back to the disco.

Marisha was still laughing when he shoved her into a chair and called a waitress to bring a cup of black coffee.

"What's up, guys?" Lilly asked, panting heavily. She had just come back from dancing with Alex. Rhonda and one of the plumbers, Ryan, had followed.

"You shouldn't let your friend roam the hallways all alone at night," Max said sternly, "especially in the shape she's in."

"What are you, her mother?" Lilly asked semi-sarcastically.

"No, I'm not her mother, but in case you've never heard, it's not wise to walk alone at night," Max said steadily. Lilly watched him walk over to the bar where the other spy was waiting for him. She sat down beside Marisha.

"Look at them . . . Max is filling his partner with the horror story of finding you in a hallway, alone. This is a resort for Pete's sake! We're under lock and key twenty-four seven, security guards everywhere! Like anyone could get to us . . . Not!" Lilly checked Marisha more closely. "Mmm . . . hmm, you're wasted, aren't you?"

"I feel fine. Look, I'm even drinking black coffee . . . spy's orders," Marisha laughed.

"Coffee? Yuk! Waitress, bring us some shooters!" Rhoda put an arm around Marisha. "This is a holiday, we're here to have fun . . . you can have coffee at home. Come on girls, let's go dance." She stood up, and held her hands out to Lilly and Marisha. "You too, Alex, get your butt on the dance floor," she ordered.

They were dancing to some rock-and-roll music. Marisha let her guard down—nothing was bothering her, nothing mattered, it was just here, just now and she felt free. The colourful blur was making her dizzy; she closed her eyes and danced slowly.

She didn't notice when the music slowed down. Her eyes opened and she saw herself standing face-to-face with Drake. He reached for her and she stepped into his arms. Pulling her close, Drake put one hand on her back, and taking her other hand in his, brought it to his mouth. After light kiss on her knuckles, he pressed her hand to his chest.

They swayed to the rhythm of the music. For the first time, Marisha saw Drake's face absent of smiles. She examined his strong chin, high cheekbones and his smouldering black eyes. When her gaze fell on his lips, she felt her pulse quicken. "What would it feel like to kiss those lips? If he bends down his head . . . and if I lift my chin just a bit, our lips will meet, and . . ."

"Marisha," Drake whispered close to her lips.

The feeling that he knew what she was thinking had made her look away. A few feet from them, she saw Lilly's arms wrapped around

Ryan's neck. His lips were on her cheek and his hands on Lilly's hips. She was envious of her friend. Lilly was a free spirit. Nothing embarrassed her; she wasn't shy, and she lived for the moment.

Drake's hand came up under Marisha's chin, and lifting her face with one finger, he forced her to look up at him. "OK?" he asked. She nodded her head. Drake put his hands on her back and Marisha found herself pressed against his chest. Reaching up, she rested her hands on his shoulders. His bow tie was gone and two top shirt buttons were open. Her nose was very close to that little triangle of dark skin framed by the fluorescent white of his shirt. His masculine scent drove her senses wild. Fighting the urge to kiss the hollow of his neck, she closed her eyes. "My God, this feels so nice . . . he feels so nice. I love the smell of his aftershave."

She had no idea how long they had been dancing, but when she opened her eyes, her face was pressed against Drake's chest, his chin was resting on top her head and there were only four couples left on the dance floor. It was hard to pull away. She would gladly have stayed in his arms for the rest of her days but the music had changed to a faster tempo and Marisha knew that she had to let him go.

Drake walked her back to the table. "Thank you," he said, looking deeply into her blue eyes. The corners of his mouth lifted in a tiny smile. He pulled out a chair for her and Marisha sat down. Wanting to thank him, she turned to where he was standing only to find him gone.

"Where did he go?" she asked. Lilly was busy saying good night to Ryan and she wasn't paying any attention to Marisha. Craning her neck, Marisha hoped to catch a glimpse of the mysterious Dracula but the only people she recognized were the two spies sitting at the bar.

"Ready to go?" Lilly's voice made her jump.

"Yeah, uh, umm, sure," Marisha stuttered.

"Now what?" Lilly quizzed.

"Nothing. Let's go."

On the way to their room, Marisha elbowed Lilly.

"Here we go again. Don't look now, but we have the spy escort behind us."

Despite Marisha's warning, Lilly turned her head. Max stopped, pretending to be interested in a painting, but the other man met Lilly's eyes. Turning to Marisha, Lilly whispered, "Something fishy about those two." As if she had told the funniest joke, both women burst out laughing.

After five tries, Lilly managed to open their room door. Kicking off her shoes and still in fits of laughter, she threw herself down on the bed.

"What the heck is that?" Marisha spotted a card hanging on the outside of the patio door. Lilly sat up.

"What's what?" Seeing the white square stuck to the window, she stopped laughing.

"What does it say?" she asked.

Marisha opened the door and reached for the paper. It was a cut out from a newspaper.

On one side was a headline of some sort. It read GIVE IT UP. Flipping the scrap to look at the other side, Marisha shrug her shoulders. "The wind probably blew it here. Look, it's nothing, really." She handed the scrap to Lilly. Examining one side, then the other, Lilly started to chuckle. "One side says, GIVE IT UP, and the other has a stock market report. Well, here you have it . . . a sign from above . . . don't play the stocks." Again, laughter had both Marisha and Lilly rolling on the bed.

"I love being drunk; everything seems wonderful and . . . and funny. I think I'll stay drunk for the rest of my life. Lilly, I want to stay here . . . I'm never going back home," Marisha laughed.

"Good idea, girlfriend. We'll marry a couple of Mexicans, get jobs at the local fish market, and live happily ever after." Lilly joined Marisha's laughter.

"Dibbs on Dracula," Marisha giggled.

"You have to help me persuade Ryan to stay in Mexico, then I'll let you have Dracula but if Ryan goes, I'm not promising anything."

Marisha threw a pillow at Lilly, missing her target by at least three feet. The laughter continued until Marisha passed out.

CHAPTER 13

"OUCH! MAN, EVERYTHING hurts! I can't comb my hair. I don't think I'll ever drink again. How do alcoholics do it?" Marisha complained.

"Stop being such a baby ... here, drink this." Lilly handed her a glass of beer with clamato juice. "Hair of the dog."

"No way! Lilly, it's ten o'clock in the morning!"

"Trust me, it will help," her friend said encouragingly.

Marisha took the glass and downed half its contents. Shivers shook her body. "I think I overdid it last night. But I must admit it sure was nice to forget all my troubles. Oh my God! I've just remembered—I danced with Dracula. I can't believe how good it felt to be held in his arms. Lilly, I think I'm in love with him ... well ... with the idea of him, anyway. I know nothing about him. He might be married.

Heck, I don't even know if he speaks English. Did you hear him speak English?"

"You know, I saw him listening to Alex's joke . . . he laughed at it, but I don't think I ever actually heard him say more than a word or two. When he speaks to Eduardo or the other bartenders, he always speaks Spanish. Hmm, I wonder, maybe he doesn't know English." Lilly shrugged her shoulders and added, "The way the other bartenders listen to him and ask him things, I think Dracula is their boss or something . . . you'd think he'd have to be able to communicate with the guests."

"You'd think," Marisha agreed.

"Hey, changing the subject, I was just looking at the patio door. You know, that paper clipping was taped to our window. See? There is a piece of tape still hanging there," Lilly pointed to the glass door. "If the wind blew it here, what's with the tape?"

"You're right, I see the tape but we're on the second floor. How would anyone get up here? And why? Just to tape a piece of paper to our window?"

Yeah, you have a point. Anyway, let's go. We'll grab something to eat and then we'll hit the beach. The ocean water will feel good," Lilly said, massaging her temples.

On the way to the beach, Lilly grabbed Marisha's elbow, "Look, there is that guy . . . the one with the binoculars." She gestured in the direction of the pool. Marisha lifted her sunglasses.

"Yeah, that's him!"

Unaware of being observed, the man propped his sunglasses on top of his head and reached for the bottle of suntan lotion. Sitting up, he began applying the lotion to his arms.

"Oh my God, isn't that . . . no!" Lilly stopped in mid-sentence.

"He almost looks like Gr . . . Greg?" Marisha stuttered in disbelief.

"That's what I thought, but no, it can't be . . . can it?"

"Christ, we haven't seen Greg for twenty-some years, who knows what he looks like now? This guy reminds us of Greg . . . that's all." Marisha didn't sound convincing. Resuming their walk, she was thinking, "There is something very familiar about the man. He could be Greg but what were the chances of that? After all those years . . . I see him in Mexico of all places? N-no . . . no way!"

The cool ocean water felt satiny smooth. Marisha floated on her back, enjoying the peacefulness and sunshine. Lilly was splashing around at the water's edge. Only a few sun worshippers came to the beach; most hung around the pools at the resort. Marisha could not understand why anyone would prefer the pool to the miles and miles of white sand, fresh, gentle breezes off the ocean and the sound of waves splashing onto the shore. She flipped onto her stomach and began a slow, lazy swim towards the shore.

"Had enough swimming?" Lilly asked, when Marisha came to stand beside her.

"I wish you could swim, it would be nice to have company in the water. You should take some swimming lessons when we get home," Marisha suggested.

"I've tried, but I don't have it in me. Some people float, some sink like a rock. I'm afraid I'm a rock," Lilly replied, laughing.

They walked over to their towels. After applying some suntan lotion, Lilly pulled a hat over her face. A minute later, she seemed to have fallen asleep. Beside her, lying on her stomach, Marisha was analyzing her obsession with Drake. She had never felt so strongly about anyone. Over the years, she thought herself in love with three different men, but never had she felt about them the way she felt about this bartender. She knew nothing about him and yet she felt somehow bonded to him. Just looking at him, being in the same room with him, had made her feel secure and happy. She wondered if there was such a thing as a soul mate. People talked about it but she had never really believed in it. Her feelings towards a stranger had her questioning whether maybe there was something to it. Otherwise, how was she to explain the blind faith she had in Drake? He could be a cold-blooded murderer, a thief, or a wife beater for all she knew, but from the first time she looked into his eyes, she felt that he was a good person. Furthermore, she knew that her search had ended . . . that she had found the part of herself that was missing from the time she was a little girl. Why had it felt so natural when she was in Drake's arms last night? Being shy, it took her a long time to let herself feel free with any men. But with Drake, it felt natural. She considered the alcohol intake. "Maybe it was the drinks. No, I felt the same about him the first day and I wasn't drunk then. I feel good just watching him, but when he looks at me, or touches me, I get a feeling that he can see right through me. Why does all the blood rush to my face when he looks at me?"

A shadow startled Marisha out of her thoughts. She sat up and was surprised to see Ryan standing next to Lilly's towel.

"I see you ladies have survived last night," he said, as he deposited his long body onto the sand. He tickled Lilly's feet. "Hey, are you sleeping?" he asked.

"I was . . . until I was so rudely interrupted." Lilly pretended to sound grumpy.

"Come on, you can't sleep this beautiful day away. We're going to see that arch," he pointed to the landmark. "Why don't you ladies come with?"

"Uh, that sounds good, what do you say, Marisha?" Lilly's voice was laced with excitement.

"I have a haircut booked in an hour, remember? But you go ahead, no use both of us missing the fun." Marisha winked at Lilly then looked up at Ryan. "Promise to take good care of my friend. She can't swim."

"We make a good team, then, neither can I," Ryan laughed.

"But boy, can we dance!" Lilly said, gathering up her towel. "Give me five minutes to change; I'll meet you by the boats, OK?"

"Lilly, wait up, I'll go to the room with you." Marisha waved to Ryan and ran to catch up with Lilly. Passing the pool, they looked in the direction where they had seen the man.

"He's gone."

"Next time we see him I'll go up and ask if he's Greg," Lilly said.

"You'll do no such thing. That's all I need . . . my past to follow me to Mexico. We came here to get away from everything and everyone, remember?"

"What if it is Greg?"

"So what? This is a free country. If he came here for a vacation, let him enjoy it. I don't want to talk to him and I'm sure he wouldn't be thrilled to see me, either."

"But . . ."

"No buts," Marisha said firmly.

After Lilly left, Marisha took a quick shower. She had a few minutes to spare before her appointment, so she took her time getting dressed. Holding a white sundress against her body, she walked towards the mirror. Not realizing how tanned she was, her own reflection surprised her. The white dress enhanced the darkness of her skin; the sun—streaked honey-blonde hair looked shiny and healthy. All of this put together made her blue eyes stand out like two sapphires. For the first time in her life, Marisha was happy with her appearance. "Great! I come all the way to Mexico to discover that I'm shallow and vain," she teased herself.

Her self-confidence added an extra spring to her step. On the way to the beauty salon, she was quite aware of the open stares and turning heads of every man she passed. She was amazed at the fact that she actually enjoyed being noticed.

Crossing the main entertainment area, she saw that the place was empty except for Eduardo and a girl, setting up coffee pots and filling the ice machine. As Marisha neared the bar, Eduardo let out a low whistle and mumbled something in Spanish. Out of the corner of her eye, Marisha saw the girl smack Eduardo on the head. She couldn't help the little chuckle that escaped her lips.

The beauty salon was located in the same building as the spa. Making a mental note to come back and explore the spa the next day, Marisha followed the arrows pointing to the salon. She was greeted by a young Mexican girl, Teresa. Like most staff at the resort, Teresa presented Marisha with a great big smile. When Marisha explained to her what kind of a haircut she was looking for, Teresa's expression revealed that English was as foreign to her as Spanish was to Marisha. All Marisha wanted was a little trim and explaining it to the girl was next to impossible. Afraid that she might come out sporting a brush cut, Marisha was ready to give up. That's when Max seemed to appear out of nowhere. Using fluent Spanish, he communicated with Teresa, and then he turned to Marisha.

"I've told our young Teresa that you would like to have the ends trimmed no more than a quarter of an inch and to leave your bangs alone."

Marisha looked at him in total surprise. She would never have given him credit for knowing Spanish.

"Wow, thank you so much . . ." she started, but Max cut her off.

"No problem," he said and quickly made his exit.

Teresa spent an hour fussing over Marisha's hair. She started with a full head massage and then she washed, cut, dried and styled. By the time Marisha left the salon, she felt relaxed and happy.

She entered the main entertainment area. All the stools around the mahogany bar were empty. Seeing Eduardo and Drake bent over some papers sent a warm surge through Marisha's body. Both bartenders looked up and the ever-ready smiles spread across their faces.

"Hola, senorita." Eduardo shouted.

"Hola," Marisha replied with ease.

Drake waved and gestured for her to come to the bar. Not having anything better to do, Marisha decided that staring at Dracula would be a nice way to pass the time while she was waiting for Lilly.

"Hola, Marisha. Como esta?" Drake reached for her hand.

"Hi," Marisha replied and placed her hand in his.

Drake lifted it to his lips, his eyes never leaving hers.

"What would you like?" he asked.

Marisha could only stare at him. Her hand was still in his and she had a very hard time thinking of anything other than kissing his smiling lips.

Eduardo came up behind Drake and lifted an empty glass, waiting for her to place an order. Her eyes locked with Drake's, Marisha cleared her throat.

"Surprise me," she said.

Drake released her hand. His black eyebrows momentarily shot upwards. Taking the glass from Eduardo's hand, he set it on the bar. He turned his back to Marisha, and without a word, started to walk away. Marisha exchanged looks with Eduardo, then both stared at Drake as he walked to the end of the bar, rounded the corner, and came to stand in front of Marisha. He turned her stool to face him and without warning, took her face in his hands, tilted her head backwards, and kissed her with such passion that Marisha was positive her heart was going to beat its way out of her chest. Then he let her go, walked back around the bar, came to stand in front of her, and leaning slightly towards her, he asked,

"Surprised?"

Seeing the look on Marisha's face, a huge grin spread across his face. "Now, about that drink?" he asked.

Not sure if she wanted to laugh, cry or run, Marisha found her voice.

"Gin!" she almost shouted.

"Make that two." Rhoda hopped on the stool next to Marisha. "Flying solo today? Where is your friend, Lilly?" she asked.

"She's gone touring with the boys from Texas." Marisha was grateful for the distraction. "Where is Alex?"

"My husband is sleeping off his hangover. He doesn't want to admit that he is not a young buck any more and that his body can't take the abuse it took a few years ago. He tries to prove to me that I'm the only one getting older, but as you see, I'm winning." Drake set the drinks before them. He smiled at Rhoda and winked at Marisha.

"He is so cute . . . don't you just want to mess up that perfect hair of his?" Rhoda spoke loud enough for Drake to hear her. He chuckled and walked away.

"I find all Mexicans are cute. It's the colouring, I think." Marisha was glad that Rhoda had joined her. After the stunt Dracula had pulled, she didn't think she'd be brave enough to stick around but neither did she want to leave.

"I think it's their eyes. Hmmm, that Drake, he's a little bit different though . . . taller." Rhoda studied the bartender before turning her attention back to Marisha. "Last night, I was watching you two on the dance floor . . . you have chemistry. I think he likes you." Seeing Marisha's face turn pink, Rhoda presented her with a knowing smile. "Well, well, well, I see he's not the only one with a crush."

"Isn't it silly? I feel like a teenager. Something pulls me to this man . . . against my better judgment I must say. Funny thing though, it feels so natural, I'm not even fighting it," Marisha confessed with a sigh.

"Some things are meant to be. Maybe he's meant to be for you," Rhoda said.

"Oh no, there is no man meant for me. I've tried a few times, but the bottom line is that I'm alone and always will be alone," Marisha said sadly.

"Why do you say that? You're beautiful and smart. Why wouldn't you want to get married, start a family and live happily ever after?"

"It's not that I didn't want to . . . it's complicated, besides, it's too late now . . ."

"It's never too late." A male voice startled both Rhoda and Marisha. Spinning around, they saw Ryan and Lilly approaching the bar. "What are we talking about, anyway, too late for what?" Ryan inquired.

"Oh, nothing. How was the tour?" Not sure how much of the conversation had been overheard by the newcomers, Marisha felt herself blush.

"You have no idea! We have to go and spend a whole day there, Marisha. What a place! The beach is perfect and the birds and animals are amazing. We watched sea lions sleeping on the rocks and schools of colourful fish swam under our boat. It was great." Lilly's tanned face was beaming. Marisha saw Ryan looking at her friend with admiration. She didn't blame him. Lilly looked absolutely gorgeous.

"How was your day?" she asked Marisha.

"Got a haircut thanks to Max, then I came here for a drink. Rhoda joined me, so here we are, drinking and chatting."

"What about Max? What did he have to do with your haircut?" Lilly looked puzzled.

"I'll tell you later."

Drake came to take Ryan's order and Marisha was too preoccupied with watching him to be bothered with explanations of her encounter with the spy.

Before long, the other Texans, a couple of plumbers and Alex came to join the party around the bar. At someone's suggestion, plans were made for everyone to meet at a nightclub downtown. Marisha's heart sank at the thought that she wouldn't see Drake until the next day. She'd be happy to stay at the resort but she wasn't given a choice to voice her opinion because Lilly accepted the invitation for the both of them. It was agreed that at nine o'clock that evening, everyone would meet at the front entrance of the resort and the transport arrangements would be made at that time.

CHAPTER 14

F ROM THE WINDOW of the minivan, Marisha studied the outskirts of Cabo San Lucas with interest. The road they were travelling on was lined with rows of colourful houses, yucca plants, cactuses and tall palm trees. The view and the Mexican music playing in the van brought a smile to her lips. She was imagining herself walking down this street with Drake, holding hands, laughing, exploring the city.

Lilly, Ryan and four other occupants of the taxi were chatting about the trip they took to the rock and about their expectations of the nightclub. Marisha sat quietly, thinking and daydreaming. Her feelings for Drake had her worried. After all, she had made a promise to herself that after what had happened with Brian, she would never so much as look at another man.

"Get a load of that! Wow, this place looks awesome!"

Lilly's excitement brought Marisha out of her daydreams. Looking in the direction of Lilly's pointing finger, she noticed that their taxi had pulled up in front of an elegant nightclub. The building stood alone, separated from others by a lush landscape filled with small palm trees and flowering shrubs. Skilfully placed spotlights shone from beneath low bushes and from under the staircase, throwing great shadows and accenting the oversized, carved doors of the front entrance. Two tuxedo-clad doormen greeted every guest and hurriedly pulled open the massive front doors.

"Look for Rhoda and Alex. They left before us, and maybe if we're lucky they have found a table," Ryan said, guiding Lilly and Marisha through the crowded club. The music was loud and the nightclub packed with people. Bouncing strobe lights made it almost impossible to see. Alex appeared in front of them.

"Over here, we have a table." He gestured towards the corner of the room. "What a crowd! We came just in time to grab the last place available. Are the others here too?" Alex was almost yelling.

"They were in a taxi behind us; should be here shortly," Ryan yelled back.

As the women sat down, Alex waved to the passing waitress. She either didn't see him or totally ignored him.

"Looks like we have to fend for ourselves," Alex gave up.

"That's okay, I'll go get us some drinks," Ryan offered.

"I'll go with you." Lilly jumped up from her chair. They disappeared into the crowd. When they came back with a tray full of drinks, the rest of their party was with them.

"I'm not sure, but I think I saw that guy, you know, the one that looks like Greg," Lilly whispered to Marisha.

"Where?" Marisha asked, looking around.

"By the bar. I didn't get a good look though; he was too far away. Let's go and check him out." Lilly took Marisha's hand and pulled her to her feet. "We'll be right back," she shouted over her shoulder in Ryan's direction.

They made their way through the maze of people. Reaching the bar, Lilly pointed to the place where she saw the mystery man.

"He was right there."

"Well, he's not there now. Let's walk around; maybe we'll run into him," Marisha suggested. They walked around the club, but the man they were after was nowhere to be seen. Reaching their table again, they gave up the search.

With the men outnumbering the women three to one, Lilly and Marisha spent a great deal of time on the dance floor. The music was great, the company fun, and time flew by. Marisha was surprised when she looked at her watch and saw it was ten minutes past midnight. Time wasn't the only surprise that night. Her chin had dropped when, all of a sudden, Drake surfaced next to her and asked if she'd dance with him.

"Oh my! What . . . what are you doing here?" she stuttered.

"I heard you were coming here tonight. I thought I'd drop in and see you . . . hope you don't mind." Drake sounded shy.

"Of course not, it's a pleasant surprise." She was looking at him, quite pleased with herself that the words came out with ease. "That's more like it. For change, I don't sound like a babbling fool when I'm talking to him." Marisha heaved sigh of relief.

"Shall we?" Drake took her by the hand and led her to the dance floor.

Dancing a couple of feet apart, Marisha had a chance to take in his appearance. Gone were the tuxedo, snow-white shirt, and bow tie. Drake looked very different in a yellow shirt and brown slacks. With an unruly strand of hair falling over his forehead, he looked less business-like and more approachable.

With the loud music, it was impossible to carry on any conversation. That suited her just fine. Just dancing and looking at him filled her heart with joy. Every time their eyes met, Drake gave her a smile that made her heart skip a beat. "God! I want the music to slow down so I can hold him. I wish I could walk up to him, wrap my arms around his neck, and kiss his smiling face till the cows come home," she thought. The music changed, but the tempo was still fast. "Just my luck, they will probably play fast songs for the rest of the night. Rats!" Marisha cursed under her breath. Drake's black eyebrows met closer over the bridge of his nose. He was studying her facial expression and looking puzzled. Marisha felt herself blush. "I swear he can read my mind!" Drake came closer and extended his hand. She took it, and they walked back to the table.

"Well, look what the cat dragged in! If it isn't Mr. Dracula himself," Lilly winked at her friend. "Where did you find him?" She grabbed Drake's chin. "You are so cute."

"Sorry, man, Lilly has had a couple of tequilas too many." Ryan pulled Lilly's hand away from Drake's face. Marisha couldn't believe her eyes. Drake looked as though he was actually enjoying the scene.

"No worries." He patted Ryan on the shoulder, then raised his hand and snapped his fingers. "Maria!" he shouted at the waitress.

"Drake, como estas, amigo." Maria smiled at Drake with a pair of very attractive dimples. Drake spoke to her in Spanish, to which Maria replied "Si," and left.

"Drake, my friend, you've got to teach me that trick. I've been trying to get her attention all night, and nothing. You snap your fingers and she comes running." Alex was impressed.

"Ah, you have to have connections . . . a cousin working as a waitress helps too." Drake clicked his tongue. Both men shared a hearty laugh.

Maria came back with a tray full of drinks and shooters. Drake paid for the order and raised his glass in a toast.

"To my new friends."

"Here, here!" Alex and Ryan raised their glasses.

"Thanks Drake . . . or as you'd say, gracias," Lilly joined in the salute.

"To new friends," Marisha contributed.

The party carried on until three o'clock in the morning. Marisha enjoyed herself tremendously. After a couple of drinks, Drake became very talkative and entertaining. He asked Marisha to dance quite often but the songs were fast and to Marisha's dismay, they were forced to dance apart. It wasn't until the final song of the night that she got her wish. Smiling, Drake took her in his arms and holding her tight to his chest, waltzed with her even when the music had stopped. Marisha loved the feeling of being held so close. She inhaled Drake's masculine scent, felt his warmth through his thin shirt, and felt his lips touching the top of her head. She wanted to lift her face to his, wanted him to kiss her on the lips, but her courage failed her. With a final kiss on her forehead, Drake put her at arm's length and looked into her eyes. A slow, knowing smile played in the corners of his mouth. Marisha's throat went dry. She moistened her lips with the tip of her tongue and swallowed hard. Drake lowered his head and for a split second she was sure that he was going to kiss her. It was a huge disappointment when for a brief moment he rested his forehead on hers, then put his arm around her shoulder, spun her around and led her back to the table.

"Party's over, kids." Rhoda was holding her husband in an upright position, ready to take their leave. Alex was swaying on unsteady legs. "My dear husband can barely remember his name, and I don't know how much longer I'll be able to hold him up. Boys, I need help getting him into a taxi." She looked pleadingly at the plumbers.

"Sure thing Rhoda, hey Bruce, grab Alex's other arm, we'll walk him outside. Let's go Alex." Two men from the plumbers' convention took Alex's arms and swung them over their shoulders. They led the procession to the waiting string of taxis parked just outside the club. Ryan had his hands full with Lilly, who insisted that there was no hurry to go back and that they should have another drink. Marisha and Drake brought up the rear. Holding hands and laughing at the sorry state of some members of their party, they congratulated each another for being able to drink them all under the table. Once they were outside, Drake asked,

"It's a beautiful night tonight; do you feel like walking back to the resort?" Marisha thought for a minute.

"Isn't it too far to walk?"

"Three-and-a-half kilometres, you're right, it is too far to walk," he answered.

"But it is a nice night. How about we walk part way and if my legs give out, we'll flag a taxi?" Marisha liked the idea of a moonlit stroll.

"OK, but promise you'll let me know when you had enough. Deal?"

"Deal." Marisha promised.

Ryan and Lilly were already seated in a taxi. Drake told them that he and Marisha were going to walk. Ryan winked and closed the taxi door. Lilly rolled down the window.

"I want to walk too." She sounded like a pouting little girl.

"Not tonight Lilly, I promise we'll go for a long walk ..."

The cab pulled away and Marisha didn't hear the rest of Ryan's promise.

"We can walk along the main road or down the path along the beach—your choice."

Drake tucked Marisha's hand under his arm and waited to hear her preference.

"How could we get a taxi if we walk by the water?"

"We can cut through any resort and be back on the main street again."

"In that case, I'd like to walk by the beach." Marisha made up her mind.

Drake gave her hand a squeeze. "I have to warn you though, the only lights out there are those coming from the resorts. It will be quite dark in places. You're not afraid to be alone with me?" he asked teasingly.

"Should I be afraid of you?" The tone of Marisha's voice matched his.

Drake didn't answer. He gave her hand another squeeze, winked at her, and with a chuckle, led her down the street away from the downtown area. The sidewalk was uneven, some of the concrete had chipped away, and Marisha had to hold firmly to Drake's arm. She thanked her lucky stars that she'd chosen her comfortable sandals and not her usual dancing shoes. It wouldn't be easy walking down those sidewalks wearing high heels.

"Penny for your thoughts" Drake's voice broke the silence.

"I'm just thinking how nice and warm the nights are. Does it ever get cold here?"

"Si, sometimes it gets very cold and windy. This time of the year, the nice weather is almost guaranteed but another couple of months and you never know."

Marisha thought about what he said. It sounded as if he had lived here for some time. She wondered if it would be appropriate to ask him some personal questions. She knew nothing about the man beside her, yet she felt as though she knew everything. One question was burning inside her—Why did she feel so secure with a total stranger? She knew that back in Canada, she'd never take a walk at this time of night down a dark path with a man she didn't know. But then, back in Canada, she had never felt this way about any man, not even the ones she was going to marry.

"You are very quiet, Marisha. If you're having second thoughts about this walk, we can still call a taxi." He looked at her with concern.

"I'm sorry. I don't mean to be bad company. Just thinking about Lilly, and wondering if she's okay." It was an outright lie and Marisha regretted it the moment it came out of her mouth. In truth, she hadn't given Lilly a second thought since she saw the cab drive away but telling Drake the truth was not an option.

"Don't you worry; Ryan will take good care of your friend. I bet she's safe and sound in her bed, right now." He added as an afterthought, "Alone."

"Yeah, you're right. Ryan wouldn't take advantage of Lilly." Marisha wanted to put that part of their conversation behind. Drake made it easy.

"Last chance to change your mind—we have to go between those two buildings to reach the beach path. It will be about a kilometre before we get to the first resort," he warned.

"I'm good to go, really," Marisha assured him.

He bent his head to look into her eyes. "De acuerdo, let's go." They walked across a grassy area between a church and something that could have been a store. The city lights disappeared behind them. As they passed the buildings, they heard some Mexican music playing in the distance. By the time they reached the pathway, the music was drowned out by the sound of waves crashing onto the shore. A gentle breeze coming from the ocean fanned Marisha's skin. Lifting her face towards the sky, she took a deep breath.

"I can't believe how beautiful this place is. You're so lucky to live here," she said.

"Where are you from, Marisha?" Drake asked.

"Canada."

"I know you come from Canada, but were you born there?"

"No, I was born in Poland, but I have lived most of my life in Canada. How about you? Were you born in Mexico?"

"In Venezuela."

"When did your family move here?"

"My parents are still in South America."

"You came here alone?"

"After college, I studied in the States. Then I came to Mexico."

From his short answers, Marisha concluded that he didn't like to talk about himself but she wasn't ready to give up just yet.

"Have you always worked as a bartender?"

"Now and again," Drake chuckled.

She didn't see any humour in her question and his chuckle puzzled her.

"Why are you laughing?"

Dodging her question, Drake pointed to the resort they were approaching.

"You should come for a tour of this place. The owner of this hotel is known for his unique décor ideas. Since you're in that business, you might find it interesting."

"How do you know what I do for living?" Marisha looked at him, surprised.

"I have my ways of finding out what I want to know," Drake told her.

"What else do you know about me?" Marisha's anxiety level shot up.

"Let's see—you were never married; you and Lilly work in the same office building and live in the same apartment block. Recently, you cancelled a wedding . . ."

"Wow! How do you know all this? Did Lilly tell you?"

"No."

Marisha stopped walking. "Drake, this isn't fair. I know nothing about you, and you seem to know everything about me. Please, if Lilly didn't tell you, then who did you talk to about me? Tell me," she pleaded.

"I had a chat with Max."

"Max! I don't know Max. What's more important, Max doesn't know me! He couldn't tell you all this. Neither Lilly nor I ever talk to Max. He's always around, we say hello, but we never ever talked to him . . . especially about our personal affairs."

"Marisha, calm down, I'm sorry. I guess it was wrong of me to go asking questions about you. In my defence though, I really like you and I needed to know if you're free. Max saw me looking at you and bugged me about it; you know . . . the guy thing. When I told him that I was hoping you were single, he told me that you were and he told me about your relationship with Lilly." Drake took her hand in his and resumed walking.

"But how does he know?" Marisha was nervous.

"I don't know. I assumed you guys knew each other from home."

"Max was on the plane coming here, but I never saw him before that."

Drake shrugged his shoulders.

"What can I tell you? Maybe he talked to Lilly."

"No, she would've told me."

Involuntary shivers run down Marisha's back. Drake put his arm around her and pulled her closer.

"Cold?" he asked.

"No, just freaked out. This whole thing is creepy."

"No use worrying about it. Talk to Lilly; maybe she had a drink with him or maybe Ryan said something. Lilly and Ryan are friends, so I'm sure she tells him some personal stuff about herself and since you're best friends, she must talk about you, too."

"I never thought about that. You're right, Ryan must have told him." Marisha calmed down. She was far too paranoid, but with everything that was going on in her life, who could blame her?

"Anyway, now it's my turn to ask you some questions. I want to know things about you too," she told him.

"Do you now? What kind of questions would you like to ask me?"

"Oh, I don't know . . . things like . . . whether you are married, how old you are, what you do when you're not bartending . . ."

Drake turned his head and looked over his shoulder.

"I have a feeling that we're being followed but every time I look, nobody's there."

They were in front of a resort now. Despite the late hour, a few people were still sitting around a fire pit. Marisha was fascinated with the view. The glare of the fire beneath the palm trees had sent shadows bouncing against the building walls, creating an illusion of a stage filled with dancers. A few seconds passed before she could tear her eyes away.

"One of these days, Lilly and I will come and have a coffee here. I would like to see the inside of this place." She turned her head for a final look.

"How about dinner tomorrow, er . . . today . . . later . . . you know what I mean." Drake didn't sound very sure of himself.

"Are you trying to ask me out to dinner, Drake?"

"Si."

"How about your job? Can you take time off?"

"Si."

"In that case, yes, I would love to come here for dinner with you."

Marisha couldn't believe how excited she was. Drake had asked her out to dinner, nothing more, but she couldn't think of anything that would make her happier. Time was precious. Two weeks would go by quickly and she wanted to spend as much time with this man as she could.

"Thank you Drake," she whispered.

"For what?" Drake sounded a bit surprised.

"For this walk, for coming to the club tonight, for being here with me, and . . ." The rest of her words went unspoken as Drake spun around pulling her with him.

"Did you hear that?" he asked.

"I didn't hear anything." Marisha strained her eyes to see through the darkness.

"I have an idea. Let's go." He took her hand, and pulled her off the pathway.

"Take off your shoes," he ordered.

"Why?" Marisha found his request surprising.

"We'll run up there." Drake pointed to the clump of palm trees between the resort they had just passed and the next. "It'll be easier to run barefoot."

"OK." She slipped her sandals off and waited for Drake to remove his shoes and socks.

The sprint through the sand wasn't as easy as she expected. Their feet sank into the sand up to the ankles, making the next step difficult. Marisha was grateful for Drake's strong arm helping her to move forward. They reached their destination and collapsed onto a wooden bench. Looking at her surroundings, Marisha whispered,

"What is this place?"

"Park," Drake whispered back. Then he put a finger to his lips. "Shhhhh . . ."

Putting his arm around her shoulder, he pointed to the pathway. In less than a minute, two dark figures emerged from the shadows. From their observation point, Drake and Marisha watched two men walking down the path in silence. They stopped and looked around. The taller man leaned towards the shorter one but whatever he was saying couldn't be heard over the crashing waves.

"The spies," Marisha whispered, recognizing the two men.

"What?"

"That's Max and his friend."

"Oh, I see. Yeah, you're right. I guess they're walking back to the resort, just like us. Well, mystery solved. I thought there was someone behind us, but I didn't see them."

Marisha pulled her feet onto the bench.

"Ooh, this feels good." She rubbed her ankles.

"Your feet are sore, aren't they? I think we'll call a cab from the next hotel."

"No, I like walking. Besides, aren't we almost there?"

"Almost . . . ours is the fourth one," Drake pointed to the lights.

"That's not far. We can walk . . . unless you prefer not to."

Taking a cab would end this night too quickly for Marisha's liking. Her feet did hurt, but she'd walk to the end of Mexico, right now, if Drake would walk with her.

"Bueno, we'll rest for a bit then we'll keep on walking."

Drake turned Marisha so her back rested against his chest. Wrapping his arms around her tightly, he rested his chin on top of head.

"How is that? Comfy?" he asked.

"Very," Marisha answered dreamily. After a short silence, she shifted her weight to one side so she could see his face. "You didn't answer any of my questions," she laughed accusingly. Drake loosened his hold and repositioned his arms, capturing her in an embrace. His eyes met hers and that heart-stopping smile spread across his face. Being just an inch or so away, Marisha could feel his breath on her lips. Her mind went blank. Nothing mattered any more. The sound of ocean waves was mild in comparison to the thunder of her heart waiting for Drake to lower his head and kiss her. His head was coming closer and closer. She could feel his lips touching hers but he was not kissing her, he was still smiling. Unable to control her longing any longer, she threw her arms around his neck and crushed her lips against his. The crazy, unexpected love she felt for this man soared through her. Drake teased her for few seconds and smiled against her eager mouth before he deepened the kiss. Placing one hand under her knees, with one swift move, he lifted her onto his lap. His hands were in her hair; his mouth was exploring and demanding, bruising her lips one minute, and soft as a feather the next. Marisha's hands went exploring. She felt the silky-rough texture of his black hair, the soft, warm skin of his neck and then she slid her hands under his shirt. Drake's muscles tensed as her fingers ran up and down the bare skin of his back. She was aware of his fullness beneath her and she knew the consequences but her own urge was just as strong. On the bench, under the blanket of Mexican sky, Marisha made love to a man who had captured not only her heart but also her very soul.

CHAPTER 15

ONE WEEK OF their vacation was gone and, to Lilly's dismay, so was Ryan. She dragged herself around the room, in no mood for any activity. It was hard for Marisha to watch her friend's suffering. She was totally lost without her constant companion. For the past few days, Lilly and Ryan had become inseparable. They were good for each other, too. Sharing the same devil-may-care attitude, they explored their tropical surroundings, closed every nightclub they were at, walked every walkway in the area, had sex in places no one else would dare, and considerably lowered the tequila supplies at the Tropical Palace. But like the majority of the tourists, the boys from Texas had come to Mexico for one week and now they were gone. The plumbers were gone; Alex and Rhoda were gone too. Knowing the people for only seven days shouldn't have made the good-byes very difficult, but it did. They were all a part of a package, the fun bunch around the bar, the gang.

"Lilly, let's go and see the new arrivals. We can show off our gorgeous tans and make them jealous. Remember how fluorescent we were when we first got here?" Marisha tried to get Lilly out of the room and doing something.

"You go, I'm going to take a nap . . . I'm tired," Lilly yawned. She crawled under the covers and pulled the blanket over her head, putting an end to further conversation.

Marisha took a bottle of water from the fridge and made her way to the balcony. Finding a little triangle of shade in the corner, she dragged a chair and footstool out of the sun and made herself comfortable. She looked towards the ocean. Seeing the aqua-blue water every day for the past seven days hadn't lessened her appreciation of the view. The palm trees, flowering shrubs, white sand and the ocean made the most beautiful picture. She could spend hours upon hours staring at the view spread before her. Many years ago, she thought that she had loved her birth country, Poland. With endless rolling farmlands, small villages and little cities and as poor as it was in comparison with the riches of Canada, it was dear to her heart. It was her country, her home. After her parents had passed away and fate took her across the world to Edmonton, she came to like that city too and made it her new home. But Mexico was a totally different experience. It was as though she had entered some magical twilight zone. She felt a strange sense of belonging. Yes, Mexico had gotten her heart. Once again, her fate had taken her on a voyage to what seemed was her final destiny. She felt that she had come home at last.

From the first time she laid eyes on Drake, she knew that she had found her reason for being. She was born to love him. Drake was her soul mate.

Everything happened for a reason, she was a strong believer in that, and now there was no doubt in her mind. Her fate made her leave Poland and stopped her marrying anyone in Canada. All this time, she had been destined to come to yet another country where the other half of her heart was patiently waiting for her.

Spending every day with Drake, going to dinners, sightseeing, taking long walks on the beach and making love, everything felt so natural and so comfortable that it had to be destiny. It wasn't only her feeling. Drake confessed that he too felt the same connection. He wasn't forthcoming with information about himself, but he had no problem telling her how he had felt when he saw her for the first time. "When I saw you, I thought—oh, there is—and then my mind went blank. You looked so familiar, so dear, it was as if I'd missed you for so long and there you were, back in my life again. Of course, that's ridiculous. If I had met you before, I would never have forgotten. It is impossible to explain but I know that you and I belong together. I've told my grandma how I feel about you and she told me that there was a reason, a good reason. According to her, we were lovers in our past lives." Drake had made that speech after their first dinner date. They were sitting on the same bench they had made love the night before.

"Simple, just like that! Drake and I love each other. I love Mexico, no hay problema, as my Latino lover would say." Marisha didn't want to think ahead. There was one more glorious week of fun in the sun before she had to face reality and reality wasn't simple at all.

"Marisha!"

Lilly's frantic cry had Marisha flying out of her chair and through the patio door.

"Lilly, what is it?" She saw her friend standing by the door, holding a piece of paper. Lilly held the white square up, enabling Marisha to see the message. In big block letters one side, the note read TRASH. On the other side, LEAVE THE MEXICAN ALONE!

"Where did that come from?"

"I heard someone by our door. I looked up and saw this thing being shoved under the door. Whoever put it there took off like a jet. It took me only a second to open the door but there was nobody in the hallway."

"I'm calling security." Marisha headed for the phone.

"No!!!" Lilly grabbed her by the arm. "We have to think before we act."

"What is there to think about? I want to know who wrote this." Marisha shook the note.

"What the hell? I'm calling . . ."

"What if . . . what if . . ." Lilly had a hard time finding words to say her thoughts.

"What are you thinking? For Christ's sake, Lilly, out with it!"

"What if Dracula is married and his wife is onto you?"

"What the hell are you talking about? Drake is not married!"

"How do you know for sure? Who else would care if you're seeing him? What do you really know about him? You've said yourself that he never answers your questions."

"He doesn't like to talk about himself, that's all."

"But why not? Has he something to hide? All those secrets are making me uncomfortable. He won't join you for dinner at the main restaurant; he takes you dancing to another resort or downtown. Yesterday, I met him by the front desk and asked him why we don't see him at the main bar any more but he didn't answer me," Lilly said sharply.

"He said that he was needed somewhere else for couple of days," Marisha explained.

"He's a bartender for heaven's sake. Where else but the bar would he be needed? Have you seen him working any bar in the last day or two?"

"No, but we haven't seen Eduardo, either. Who knows what else they do? Maybe they work some private functions."

"If that's the case, why wouldn't he say so?"

"I don't know. I don't think he has a wife running around this resort, composing notes to me either," Marisha said with conviction.

"Up to you, but I don't think you should make a big deal out of this piece of garbage." Lilly threw the note onto the desk. "What would security do, anyway?"

"You're right. I'll show this to Drake and see if he has any ideas."

"I wouldn't do that. You like the guy, so have fun with him. We're here for one more week and that's that. What's the point of dragging confessions out of him? If he thinks of himself as your holiday boy-toy, let him. After we leave, you'll never see him again."

The words coming out of Lilly's mouth had a sour note to them. Marisha knew that her friend was referring more to her brief romance with Ryan than hers and Drake's. But Lilly's words hit Marisha hard. Not only the prediction of the bleak future, but also the possibility of Drake being a fake, a cheap thrill seeker, had punched the air out of her lungs. She gave herself to him, trusted him unconditionally. She was in love with him. Was it all a mistake?

"Let's go have something to eat. I'm starving," Lilly suggested.

"Whatever!" Marisha snapped.

"Hey! Don't bite my head off. If you don't want to eat, say so."

"Never mind . . . sorry. Yeah, I'm hungry too." Marisha managed a smile.

The main restaurant was filled with the excited faces of new arrivals. Marisha and Lilly chose a table in a far corner. Not having much of an appetite, both picked at their food with little interest.

"I think we should get drunk tonight." Lilly lifted her glass to summon the waiter.

"What would that solve?" Marisha wanted to know.

"It might numb the pain."

"Until tomorrow. Then what? We can't stay drunk for the rest of our lives." Marisha reasoned. In truth, she was thinking about getting drunk too. Drake was gone today. He had told her that he had to attend to some business and he'd call her the next day.

After the meal, Marisha and Lilly went for a short walk around the grounds and on the way back, stopped by the bar. Two new bartenders and a new clientele greeted them with friendly smiles. It was sad not to see the familiar faces.

"Hey, look over there. Isn't that Max and his side-kick?" Lilly pointed to the table by the stage. "Well, what do you know, they're still here."

"Great. Of all the people I would like to see here, it had to be those two," Marisha said sarcastically.

Lilly hopped onto a stool and ordered couple of gin and tonics.

"To hell with the world, let's have a good time tonight. I miss Ryan so much that it hurts, but what can I do? I knew he was here for only a week. I should have prepared myself for his departure. But no, not me! I had to go and fall for the shmuck that lives half a world away. Life sucks!" Lilly touched her glass to Marisha's. "Salute."

"At least you knew where you stood with him. I don't even know if Drake is married. Maybe he's at home right now with his wife and kids." With the determination of a sailor, Marisha emptied her drink.

"Senor, por favor." She lifted her glass for a refill.

"A mi tambien," Lilly joined her.

At ten o'clock, they went to the disco. The place wasn't the same without the Texans and the plumbers. Even the bartenders were different. But the music was good, and after a couple more drinks, Lilly pulled Marisha to the dance floor. Two sets later, they abandoned the dance floor in favour of another drink.

"They're playing our song," said a voice above their heads. Lilly turned around so fast she lost her balance. A pair of strong arms steadied her, then lifted her up in the air. She was squealing with joy as she dangled above Ryan's face. He brought her halfway down and she wrapped her arms around his neck.

"Ryan, I thought you were gone," she managed between the kisses.

"I was, but when we landed in Dallas, I knew I had to come back so I bought another week and here I am." Ryan showered Lilly with kisses.

Marisha watched as the pair made their way to the dance floor. Despite the fast music, they were dancing close, their bodies moulded together and their lips locked in a kiss. She was happy for Lilly. Finishing her drink, Marisha left the disco.

Wrapped in a housecoat, she sat on the balcony and analyzed the events of the day. That horrible note slipped under their door had not been mentioned since they left the room. Lilly didn't think it was worth worrying about it and Marisha didn't want to bring it up. She was holding it in her hand now, looking at the offensive scrap of paper and thinking of the person who had gone to the trouble of writing and delivering it. Could Lilly be right? Did Drake have a wife, or perhaps a jealous girlfriend? He was a very attractive man. Why wouldn't he have someone? Then there was the question of his employment. He hadn't worked in the main bar since the day he had joined the party at the downtown nightclub. Was he fired? If that was the case, should she feel bad? It was well known that the staff at the resorts didn't make big money. If Drake lost his job because he got involved with a tourist, how was he going to survive? Maybe his boss had slipped her the note. But why be so rude about it? Why not read her the riot act about rules and regulations, and be done with it.

She needed some answers, that was for sure, but how was she to go about it? Asking Drake point blank could embarrass him. He hadn't told her anything about himself, so she couldn't accuse him of lying to her. He didn't exactly have to twist her arm to have sex with him; she practically seduced him. "What will I tell him when he phones tomorrow . . . if he phones, that is! What a mess. How do I get myself into these things?"

"Maybe I should show this paper to security. No! Lilly's right, what would they do about it? They'd most likely tell me to leave Drake alone and that would be embarrassing." Marsha's head started to hurt. It was no use. Even the nasty note and Drake's secrets didn't change the way she felt about him. All she had to do was close her eyes and there he was, stirring her emotions with his half-shy smile, seeing right through her with those beautiful black eyes of his.

She didn't want to believe that he was capable of pretending that he cared for her as much as she did for him. It was impossible to fake the passion they'd shared. She saw with her own eyes the effect her touch had on him. When they made love, he cried her name among some Spanish words she didn't understand. The way he'd kissed her, looked at her, he wasn't pretending.

CHAPTER 16

S HE WOKE UP to the sound of laughter coming from the grounds below. It was daylight and a few people were already splashing in the pool. Checking her watch, Marisha was surprised to see it was 8 a.m. Cursing herself for falling asleep in the chair, she struggled to an upright position. Every muscle in her body screamed with pain, and her head was pounding. "Hot shower, I need a hot shower." Limping and moaning, she made her way to the bathroom. Passing by Lilly's empty bed, she had to smile. "You lucky dog," she thought. The ringing phone made her flinch. Rubbing her temples, she walk to the apparatus and lifted the receiver.

"Hello?"

"Buenos dias Marisha, como estas?" Drake's friendly voice came over the lines.

"Drake, I'm fine, how are you?"

"I've missed you. Have you had your breakfast yet?"

"No, I'm about to have a shower."

"Hurry up. I'll pick you up by the front entrance in an hour."

"Where are we going?"

"It's a surprise. Bring your bathing suit."

"But . . ."

"Hasta luego." Drake hung up.

One hour wasn't much time. Marisha winced with every step she took towards the shower, but her heart was singing with joy. She'd missed Drake yesterday and could hardly wait to see him. All the doubts and worries were gone, replaced with the anticipation of spending time with the man of her dreams.

After drying her hair, she tied it in a ponytail. Putting on a pair of white shorts and a pink T-shirt, she followed Drake's request and put her bathing suit and a towel into a small beach bag. Wanting to leave a note for Lilly, she went searching for a piece of paper. Her eyes fell on the nasty note from the previous day. Picking the offensive scrap, she crumbled it and tossed it in the garbage. The decision to take one day at a time had lifted her spirits. She scribbled a note for Lilly and left the room.

Drake was waiting for her at the entrance, as promised. When she saw his smiling face, Marisha felt the familiar head-rush. She rushed into his waiting arms and he gave her a bear hug. Nothing mattered any more—the note, the doubts, nothing. Being with Drake was all it took for her to feel loved and safe. They walked towards the parking lot.

"I have rented a Jeep. We're going on a journey." Drake informed her.

"You've rented a Jeep? Isn't that expensive?" With his questionable employment, Marisha didn't want him to spend money on things he couldn't afford. From his arched eyebrows and the look he gave her, it was easy to tell that her question surprised him.

"You think I can't afford to rent a Jeep?"

"Well, can you?"

Drake tossed his head back and laughed as if she'd told him a funny joke. He opened the door and helped her inside the Jeep. Marisha noticed a blanket on the back seat, and a large basket set on the floor. Drake jumped into the driver's seat and gunned the engine.

"Are we going on a picnic?" she asked.

"Si."

"Don't you have to work today?"

"No."

The one-word answers got her thinking about the note. Was he being secretive? Did he have something to hide?

"Drake, you never really answer any of my questions," she asked accusingly.

"What questions, por Dios?"

"Are you married?"

It just had slipped out. She didn't want to ask. What if she didn't like his answer? Nonetheless, the question was out and she held her breath, waiting. Drake stepped on the brake, shifted the Jeep into park and slowly turned to her. From the expression on his face, Marisha knew that for some reason the question had offended him. He looked angry; she could see it in his tensed jaw line.

"You ask me that?" he said, none too friendly.

"Why are you angry with me? I'm just asking a simple question. Don't you think I have the right to know?" She stuck to her guns.

"I thought that we understood each other. I can't believe you'd ask ... I ... you ..."

Drake hung his head, not looking at her. Marisha didn't know what to make of his half-statement. Was she supposed to understand that they were having a holiday fling ... no ties ... no questions asked?

"Drake ..."

"Don't! I think I have made a huge mistake," Drake snapped.

He slid off the seat, came around the Jeep and opened the door. Taking Marisha by the hand, he helped her out and shut the door. He walked around the vehicle, got in and with squealing tires, left Marisha staring at the back of the Jeep disappearing down the driveway. "Wh ... what the ... what happened?" Marisha couldn't comprehend the situation. "He just drove off ... without me." Her mind was preoccupied and she hadn't noticed a car pulling out from the parking spot behind a delivery van, until it was about to hit her. She felt a vice-like grip on her arm and someone pulled her out of harm's way. Losing her balance, she leaned heavily on her rescuer.

"Thank y ..." Lifting her head, she was surprised to see the man holding her. "Max?"

"What the devil are you doing standing in the middle of the road?" He shook her. "You could have been killed, for Christ's sake!"

"Well, it looks like my guardian angel came to my rescue, again." She tried to loosen Max's grip. "I'm fine, you can let go now."

He gave her a stern look. "Answer my question!" he demanded.

"Wow, now, I don't owe you any explanations."

"Granted, but you have to be more careful. What if I wasn't here to pull you away?"

"Speaking of that . . . how is it that you're always there when I need help?"

"It's my j . . . , oh, never mind." Max shook her hand off his arm as though her touch had offended him. He turned his back and strolled away without another word.

On the way back to her room, Marisha's pride was suffering. "One man ditches me in the middle of the road, another brushes me off like I was a speck of lint on his sleeve, isn't this just great! God! This is not my day." She was angry, but more than that, she was hurt.

She didn't know Drake very well but for some reason, she'd never thought he would dump her like that . . . without any explanation. Man!

Back in her room, Marisha was surprised to see Lilly sitting on the balcony.

"You're home."

"So are you. I thought you were spending the day with Dracula."

"I thought so too, but obviously I was wrong."

"What happened? Did he stand you up?"

Marisha started to explain her morning to Lilly. Her story finished, she fell silent. Lilly took in all the information.

"I don't know . . . if he isn't married, he'd tell you. And if he wanted to have a fling, he should say so. Anyway, if he is married, and he's having a thing with you, think about what kind of man he is. Worthless piece of shit, cheating on his wife, that's what I think."

"Somehow I don't believe that. He doesn't seem the type." Marisha said half-heartedly.

"Put two and two together. The secrecy, the notes . . . sneaking around," Lilly took Marisha's hand. "You're better off forgetting him," she suggested.

"Well, a little too late for that, wouldn't you say? I can't help how I feel. I don't like it, but I can't help it." Marisha went inside and came back with couple of bottles of beer. Handing one to Lilly, she asked, "How about you, how come you're here without your permanent attachment?"

"Ryan is sleeping. We stayed up most of the night. I'm giving him some time to recoup, if you know what I mean." Lilly winked at Marisha.

"Oh, you evil brat! You're going to kill that man," Marisha teased.

"Hmmm, but what a way to go." Lilly raised her glass in a salute.

Since Marisha's plans for the day hadn't panned out, Lilly suggested that she join her and Ryan on a tour of the city churches. As much as Marisha wanted to go, she declined the offer, saying that she needed some time out with a good book. Although she didn't say it to her friend, she didn't want to intrude on the very little time the lovebirds had left. "At least one of us should have fun tonight," she thought.

CHAPTER 17

AFTER LILLY LEFT, Marisha poured a bath and book in hand, prepared to enjoy a good, long soak. The intentions were there but her mind was not complying. She read the same two paragraphs over and over and nothing was sinking in. The morning scenes were playing in her head like a movie on constant rewind. Frustrated, she threw the book across the bathroom and resting her head on the edge of the tub, allowed the tears to spill free. "Stupid! Stupid! Stupid! Why did I allow myself to fall in love again? Three times burned . . . I should have known that I'd end up like this. God! I didn't plan any of it. How am I going to live without him? Why didn't I see him for what he is? I fell for his smile, for his looks, and took it for granted that he's just as nice inside as he is on the outside." Burning tears of self-pity embarrassed her. Behaviour like that was expected of a nineteen-year old, not a woman her age.

Still cursing the luck of the Polish, she came out of the bathroom. A white piece of paper by the door stopped her short. Afraid of what the note would say, Marisha toyed with the idea of picking it up and tossing it into a wastebasket, unread. Curiosity didn't allow it. She picked up the page and looked at it. Under the hotel's logo there were just a few words, "Come to the beach at ten o'clock." No signature, no reason, just a simple request. Not recognizing the handwriting, her heart pounded with excitement. "It has to be from Drake. He wants to meet me, explain why he had left me standing in the driveway. That's it, he will apologize and everything will be OK. He cares . . ."

Her watch told her that if she was going to make it by ten o'clock, she'd better hustle. Not bothering with makeup, she dried her hair and slipped into a pair of jeans. Changing the t-shirt from white to green, and back again, her enthusiasm petered out. "Maybe he just wants to give me my beach bag back. What if he doesn't want to talk? What if . . . ?"

Key in hand, she stood in front of the door, undecided. Gathering every ounce of courage left in her body, she walked out into the hallway and firmly pulled the door shut.

"I need to know," she thought.

At ten o'clock, the beach was deserted and dark. The only lights came from the hotel and from the few torches lit around the fire pit near the lowest terrace. Marisha looked to the right, then to the left—nothing. The black ocean waves struck the beach with great force. The sky was just as black. In the daytime, everything looked colourful, tropical and inviting. At night, the same place looked dangerous and forbidding. Taking her sandals off, she started towards the clump of rocks scattered on the beach about five hundred yards past the resort. The sand felt cool on her feet. Straining her eyes in the darkness, she was positive that she could make out a figure standing by the farthest rock. Her steps quickened. The sooner she'd reach Drake, the better. It was scary to be here all alone. "Why didn't he meet me by the resort? What is he going to tell me?" The questions circled in her head. Guided only by the dark outline of the rocks, Marisha was closing the distance. Reaching the first rock, she paused and looked around. Not seeing anyone, she walked another few yards to the last rock.

"Drake, are you here?" She asked impatiently. "You've made me walk alone all this way, the least you could do is to meet me at the first rock."

"I knew you'd come. Trash like you wouldn't resist an invite for a roll in the sand, would you? What's the matter, you're disappointed that I'm not your Mexican?"

Marisha stood frozen to the spot. She recognized the man that reminded her of Greg.

"Who are you?" Her voice shook. "Nice, very nice. You've ruined my life, bitch, and now you don't recognize me?"

"Greg?"

"Oh, so you do remember."

The tone of Greg's voice frightened her. She turned to run but he grabbed her and they both fell on the sand. Marisha struggled to get free but she was no match for his strength.

"Where do you think you're going? Don't you want to stay and visit?" he spat.

"Let me go! You won't get away with this."

"Get away with what? You came here of your own free will. I didn't have to twist your arm, did I?"

"Let go or I'll scream."

"Go ahead, scream, who's going to hear you?"

"What do you want with me?"

"Just to talk, you owe me that. I've waited over twenty years to have my say and, by God, I'm going to have the floor and you're going to listen!"

Greg rolled onto his side and pulled her to a sitting position. Marisha pushed him with all her might and managed to get to her feet. He scrambled after her and in a matter of seconds had her by the arm.

"You fucking bitch, I said you're going to listen to me and you will, if I have to tie and gag you, you hear?"

Realizing the hopelessness of the situation, Marisha slumped down into the sand. "Maybe if I sit here for a while, someone will come by. If not, after I rest, I'll make a run for it." Making that decision calmed her down. Greg sat down beside her.

"That's better," he said.

"You're the one with the notes, aren't you?" Marisha asked, already knowing the answer. She needed to buy some time to plan her escape.

"Yup, I warned you. But you didn't listen."

"Greg, did you follow me to Mexico?"

"Right again."

"But why?"

"Why? She asks why? Let me see, I knew that you'd sniff out some guy here. I couldn't let it happen. I have to keep my eye on you all the time."

"I don't understand. What difference does it make to you if I'm seeing anyone?"

"What's not to understand? You've screwed up my life, so I've made it my mission to fuck up yours. Fair is fair." Greg shrugged his shoulders matter-of-factly.

"How did I screw up your life?"

"You've made a fool out of me in front of my family and friends. I have to live with that shame for the rest of my life. Do you think I'd let you have it better?"

"But that was years ago. We were just a couple of kids . . ."

"And that makes it okay?" Greg said sarcastically.

"Didn't you find anyone else?"

"How could I? I was too busy making sure you didn't."

Marisha thought about what Greg said. She looked at him and worded her next question carefully.

"Were you following me all the time, spying on me?"

"To this day!" he said. "You've denied me a normal life and I'm doing the same for you. Did you think I'd let you get married, have children, and live happily ever after? Not!"

Marisha caught her breath.

"Roman . . . did you . . . ?"

"You've got it. I told him over and over to drop you, to run while he could. The idiot wouldn't listen."

"What did you do?" Terror gripped her throat.

"I did what I had to do. The bastard fought to the end. But I won, didn't I?"

"Greg, you're sick. You need help."

"Shut the fuck up! The sooner you accept the fact that you're going to be all alone like me, the better. I'll stop you from having any kind of life or I'll die trying. No baby, you and I, we will stay single. You made a choice to be alone over twenty years ago and I'm here to make sure your wish comes true." Greg was nodding his head.

"You can't do that. Why don't you put the past behind you, and move on? Life is too short to be miserable, Greg."

"'Can't do it!' Ha! My dear, I have done it. Look at your life. No dates, no husband, no children—alone, like me," Greg said victoriously.

"But you can't watch my every step . . ."

"Can and do. Got rid of Roman, Brian, the bartender and every other scum sniffing around you, didn't I?" he replied smugly.

"Oh my God! What have you done to Drake? Answer me!" She was shouting.

"Now, that's for me to know and you to never find out," Greg laughed.

"That's it, I'm going to the police!"

Marisha bolted to her feet. Greg grabbed her from behind and pulled her to his chest. She felt the cold blade of a knife pressed against her throat.

"Oh no you don't! I'll slice you like the piece of shit you are. We're going to make a deal, right here, right now . . ."

A flood of lights lit up the beach. Marisha was blinded.

"Police! Drop the knife and let the lady go." The voice sounded familiar.

"Back off, or I cut her." Greg tightened his grip and Marisha felt the knife cutting the skin on her jaw.

"Don't do anything stupid. Let the lady go."

"Fuck off, cop." Greg stood his ground. "And get the fucking light off my face."

Marisha felt the pain under her chin. Someone jumped Greg from behind and she felt her legs give way from under her. There was a struggle. Two men pinned Greg to the ground and flipped him onto his stomach, cuffing his hands behind him. Marisha recognized Max and his friend. She watched the scene in total disbelief.

"Did he cut you?" Max knelt by her side, shining the flashlight over her face. He pulled a handkerchief from his pocket, applied pressure and held it against her jaw. "Son-of-a-bitch got you. You'll need stitches. Hang in there, Marisha. We'll get you to the hospital." Max put his free arm around her in an attempt to lift her up.

"Max, I'm fine. It doesn't hurt much. I can walk." She scrambled to her feet.

With Max's partner pushing Greg and Max half-carrying Marisha, they made their way to the resort.

Marisha couldn't remember how or when she got to the hospital. When she opened her eyes, Max was sitting by her bed.

"What happened?" she asked in a weak voice.

"You passed out before we got to the resort. Not to worry, you've lost some blood, but the cut wasn't bad . . . only three stitches under your chin."

"Greg?"

"Sean took him to the holding bin at the airport; we're all going home tomorrow."

"You're a cop?"

"Special agent, Max Parker at your service" Max produced a badge.

Marisha needed some answers, but her face hurt every time she moved her mouth.

"You're a cop . . . how? Explain, please . . ." she pleaded.

Max looked at her with pity. Her face was swollen and red and her eyes revealed how confused she was.

"OK, I guess I had better tell you everything before you rip those stitches by asking questions. Lie back down." He pulled the pillow higher behind her head and gently pushed her against it. "That's an order, young lady." For the first time, Marisha noticed that he had a nice smile.

"Your firm called us to check out a peeping Tom. It took us a week before we found him at the building across the street from your office. Other than looking through the binoculars, we had nothing on him. My partner, Sean, had a gut feeling that Greg's spying involved something more. Instead of arresting him on the spot, we made some inquiries and followed the chap around for couple of days. As it turned out, we were following him and he was following you. Yeah, he was trailing behind you everywhere. So we made some inquiries about you, too. Roman's unsolved death came up and that made Greg interesting. We traced his calls to your apartment, watched him send you flowers and saw him watching you from across the street, but he never made contact with you. I wanted to tag him as nothing more than a stalker but Sean felt that Greg was somehow involved with

Roman's sudden death. We couldn't get any proof. Then we found out that he bought a ticket to Mexico for the same time you did and that put us on the alert. He was up to something. We followed you and followed him. It was almost predictable that he'd try to talk to you here. Sean saw him slip a note under your door." Max shifted uncomfortably. "You won't like this part," he warned. "We had to see what it said, so I got into your room. Don't look so surprised, we had a passkey from day one ... security. Anyway, thankfully, you were in the bathtub. The timing was perfect; we had plenty of time to set a trap. Everything he said to you on the beach, we have on tape. Sean had a feeling that Greg was going to confess to Roman's murder. My partner has a sixth sense when it comes to murder," Max said proudly.

Marisha listened to Max's story and her mind was racing. Stuff like that happened in the movies, not in the lives of ordinary people like herself. Everything that she believed was her fate, the luck of the Polish, was nothing more than some sick-minded person's vendetta. Roman, Brian, Drake ...

"Drake, what's he done to Drake?"

Max saw the panic in her eyes. He took her hand to reassure her.

"As far as we know, Drake was called away on business. He is fine, I promise."

Marisha didn't buy his story. Drake was a bartender, if he still had a job. What kind of business could he be called to? No, Greg had done something to him, she was sure of it.

"Drake ..."

"You'll most likely see Drake tomorrow, before we leave. You'll see, he'll be at the resort, doing whatever he normally does," Max tried again.

"Leave . . . tomorrow?" "What is he talking about, we have another week here," Marisha thought. She looked at him for explanation.

"Sorry to be the party pooper, but you have to come back with us. We need you to tell your side of the story. You don't want Greg to get off on some technicality, do you?"

Max looked at her pleadingly. "Without you, the thing can go sideways. Trust me, if there was another way, I wouldn't dream of cutting your vacation time."

Marisha closed her eyes. "Great, just great! Lilly will love that."

CHAPTER 18

THE NASAL VOICE on the intercom announced the arrival of Flight 211 from Mexico. Marisha got to her feet. Two weeks had passed since she'd left Lilly in Cabo San Lucas and she was anxious to see her. Life was empty without her best friend. Lots had happened in the past few days and Marisha couldn't wait to share the news.

As the travellers were making their way to the luggage carousel, Marisha craned her head in every direction, looking for Lilly. When her friend came through the door, she waved and smiled. Marisha waved back.

"Oh, it's so good to see you. How was the flight?" Marisha's arms encircled her friend.

"Long."

Taking in Lilly's red, swollen eyes and the way she was clinging to Marisha, it was evident that the parting was heart breaking and the flight none too pleasant.

"Welcome home. I've missed you so much."

"I've missed you too." Lilly dabbed her eyes with a Kleenex.

Marisha put an arm around Lilly's shoulders and walked with her towards the carousel.

"So tell me, how was the last two weeks? How is Ryan? Where did you guys stay last week? I want to hear everything."

"After you left, I moved in with Ryan and we stayed at the Palace. Last week we found this little motel about ten kilometres from the city and we stayed there. It was the best time ever. We rented a car and every day we drove to a different spot. Man, I miss Ryan already . . . I love him so much. Can you believe it? Me, at my age, I'm in love!" Lilly hung her head. "How have you been?" she asked.

"Pissed off that I had to come back a week early and for what? Every day I had to go to the police station, then to court. You have no idea how relieved I was when they finally charged Greg. The judge threw so many charges at him that the bastard will rot in jail for a long time."

"Sorry I wasn't here for you."

"Lilly, there was no reason to spoil the vacation for both of us."

The luggage carousel turned and Lilly moved closer. Marisha admired her friend's tan. Three weeks in the tropics had turned her pale skin to golden brown. Other than the sadness in her eyes, Lilly looked healthy. "Now comes the hard part. I knew Drake for only a week, and I can't get him out of my heart. How is Lilly going to manage without Ryan? Having him for three weeks, every day, loving him, she's going to need me more than ever and I'm going to need her too."

"Where did you park?"

Lilly's question startled Marisha. "Close," she answered. Taking one bag from Lilly, she noticed a package tied to the handle. "Hey is that my beach bag?"

"Yeah, the maid brought it to the room a couple of days after you left."

"Drake . . . did you see him? Was he there?"

"We saw him a couple of times. He didn't work as a bartender though. Once, he was on the stage, saying something in Spanish, next time he was talking to the floor manager at the lobby, and another time he was walking a horse on the beach."

"A horse?" Marisha was surprised.

"Yup, a horse. Maybe they fired him from the bartending and now he's a stable boy. Who knows?" Lilly rolled her eyes.

"Did he . . . did he ever ask about me?"

"Sorry kid, he didn't even look in our direction." Seeing the pain in her friend's eyes, Lilly's voice softened. "How are you dealing with it? It's been two weeks . . . is it getting any easier?"

"It will never get easier. I'll relive that week for the rest of my life." Marisha's voice sounded strange. Lilly looked at her sympathetically.

"It will stop hurting after a while. You'll forget him."

"No I won't," Marisha said sadly.

"It feels like that now, trust me, I feel the same way, but we're going to make it, one way or another. Remember the saying—what doesn't kill us makes us stronger."

"At least you know how Ryan feels about you. Who knows, maybe you two will end up together, eventually."

"Ryan said that he'd look into transferring here. He works for an oil company. They do have a branch in Alberta, but I won't hold my breath. In the heat of the moment, people say all sorts of things. When push comes to shove, not too many keep their promises. I'm going to live my life, day by day, not expecting anything. If I have to, I'll accept the fact that I'll be alone and adjust to it. You will too, I promise."

"Maybe you'll forget, but I know I won't."

The conviction in Marisha's voice worried Lilly. Putting the luggage into the truck, she was thinking of what to say, how to reassure her, without hurting her feelings. There was no easy way. Slamming the trunk shut, Lilly leaned against it.

"Lots happened in that one week. With your crazy infatuation, Greg, and all . . . yeah, you'll probably never completely forget. But in time, your hormones will cool down, Drake will become just a memory from Mexico and you'll see him for what he really was. Before you ruin your life crying for him, think if he's worth it. What if he goes home every night to his wife and children? What if you were just a pleasant distraction in his humdrum, bar-serving life? Can't you see that if he gave a rat's ass about you, he'd have phoned you by now? I'm sorry for being a bitch, but I need you to think logically."

"How can he phone? He doesn't have my number."

"Oh, please. He could have asked me for it or looked it up in a resort's ledger. How about the Information service? If he wanted to, he'd find you. Think, Marisha," Lilly said sternly.

"But you don't understand. I . . ."

"How can you say that I don't understand? Just this morning I had to tear myself away from the greatest guy I have ever known. I can't even imagine how I'm going to survive tomorrow or the next day. So yes, girlfriend, I do understand."

"Lilly."

"What?"

"I'm pregnant!"

CHAPTER 19

"JOSH, PLEASE EAT your breakfast."

"No!"

"You have to eat, hurry up. We have no time for games today."

"No!"

Two-year-old Josh pushed his cereal bowl to the edge of the highchair. Resting his elbows on the tray, he folded his chubby little hands under his chin. With his mouth set in a stubborn pout, he challenged his mother with his eyes.

"No!"

Jenny, Josh's twin sister, pushed her bowl away too. Copying her brother, she assumed an identical position in her highchair. She looked from her brother to her mother, waiting to see where the game was going.

Marisha looked at the babies and couldn't stop herself from laughing.

"That's it, you little brats! Conspiring against your Mommy, are you?"

She watched the corners of two little mouths go up, dimpling the chubby cheeks and sending dancing sparks into their chocolate brown eyes. Putting her hands on top of their heads, she messed up their soft, black hair.

"Two against one, hmmm, what am I going to do with you? Maybe if I tickle you like this . . ." She used one hand on each baby's tummy and wiggled her fingers, sending the toddlers into a frenzy of laughter.

"No Mommy, no," Josh squealed.

"No Mommy, no," Jenny echoed her brother's protest.

"Are you going to eat?" Marisha paused, tilted her head to one side, and waited for an answer. Josh reached for his bowl, pulling it closer. As always, Jenny copied.

"Now, that's more like it." Marisha smiled.

The children made honest attempts to get some food into their mouths. Unfortunately, most of it ended up on their faces and their bibs. Now and again, Marisha spooned a mouthful, but for the most part, she let them practise feeding themselves. The sooner they learned, the easier her job would be. Two years of double-duty was taking its toll, and she was looking forward to the day when the twins would be a little more independent. She enjoyed spending all her time and energy on them now, but soon she'd have to return to work full time and she would need all the help she could get. Not that she wanted to go back to work full time, but her bank accounts looked alarmingly low. Working three days a week as she had been for the past six months didn't quite cover all the expenses. Between food, clothing, daycare and other costs, her lifetime savings were disappearing faster than she cared to admit.

Lilly's suggestion to go after Drake for child support wasn't an option. Three years had gone by and Marisha hadn't heard from him. Obviously, he had forgotten her so what was the point of hunting him down? Lilly's argument that he had a right to know that he had fathered a son and a daughter made Marisha feel somewhat guilty at first, but she had no time to dwell on it. When she was pregnant, her days were full between her job and constant visits to the doctor's office. Getting pregnant for the first time at the age of forty-three had raised all sorts of issues. After the twins were born, there were complications with Jenny's digestive system. By the time the babies were two months old, Marisha was physically and emotionally exhausted. Her only experience with children was from when she herself was a child, looking after her little cousins in Poland. Caring for two newborns at once was a real challenge.

Lilly was a godsend. After Ryan had relocated to Edmonton, his job took him into northern parts of Alberta for weeks at a time. Newlywed and alone, Lilly spent most evenings at Marisha's apartment, helping with the babies and the housework but, most importantly, giving Marisha much needed time to rest.

Forgetting Drake completely was not possible. She saw his eyes, his smile, and his sometimes-shy disposition every day in Josh and Jenny. From their dark complexion and the blackness of their hair, to the almost black eyes, the children bore a remarkable resemblance to their father.

There were times when Marisha caught herself fantasizing that she, Drake, and the twins were a happy family living together, but she had never put those fantasies into words, not even to Lilly. She never had regretted having the babies even though there was a time when fearing for her own life, the doctors had tried to convince her to terminate the pregnancy. Looking at her happy, healthy children now, she thanked God for giving her this miracle.

"OK munchkins, time to get you cleaned up and dressed. Mommy has to go to work."

Watching her friend storm through the front door of the office, Lilly burst out laughing.

"You always give the impression that someone is chasing you."

"Hi Lilly," Marisha leaned on Lilly's desk to catch her breath. "My little monsters have developed a habit of throwing a fit every time I drop them off at the daycare. I'm always running late. Do me a favour—reschedule my downtown appointment to later on this morning. I desperately need that contract, so I want to make sure all my ducks are in place, I's dotted and tees crossed."

"Okay, okay, I get the picture. And sweetie, you might want to take that Cheerio out of your hair, that's sooo last year." Lilly flexed her wrist and blinked her eyes.

"What if I tell you I'm wearing it for good luck," Marisha teased, fishing out the sticky little circle from her hair.

In the past, Marisha had prided herself on being punctual. If anything, she'd show up for an appointment with time to spare. The arrival of her little duo had somehow changed her sense of timing. She was always on the run and always couple of minutes behind.

"Don't worry ma'am, the traffic looks better ahead."

Making eye contact in the rear-view mirror, Marisha smiled at the cab driver. At this point, it really didn't matter—she was already five minutes late. Midmorning traffic wasn't usually this heavy, but since she was in a hurry, of course the luck of the Polish had to step in and complicate her life. She leaned back in her seat and relaxed. The commission from this contract would be an answer to her prayers. It wasn't just a house or a condo to decorate, it was a whole hotel. Not just any hotel, it was one of the best resort-hotels worldwide. "Dammit! If only I had left the office ten minutes earlier ... if ... oh well, no use crying over spilled milk. They'll thank me for showing up and tell me to go back to where I came from. Dammit!"

The colossal buildings of the downtown stood proud and tall against the clear sky. Passing by the CN tower in Edmonton, Marisha remembered how impressive it looked when she saw this giant for the first time. Now, still big and tall, it was somewhat dwarfed by the rest.

"Looks like there is some trouble up ahead, ma'am. If I let you out here, you'll get there faster on foot." The cabby looked at her apologetically.

"Of course there would be some trouble ahead, why not? Why would anything go smoothly, now? Dammit!"

"Thank you." She paid for the fare and gathering her briefcases, started towards the tall office building a couple of blocks away.

Suspecting that the contents of the heavy load she was carrying would never see daylight anyway, she was swearing under her breath.

CHAPTER 20

THE NESSEX INC. office building towered over the street. From top to bottom, the walls were made of tinted, mirrored glass, making it impossible to see inside. Marisha knew the building well. Four years ago, she was hired to design an office space in the building for a small modelling company. After that, she had decorated two other offices, a reception area, and a small coffee shop located on the main floor.

She paused by the front door. Her reflection was startling. Wind-blown hair, wrinkled skirt, and with her handbag pulling the shirt off her shoulder, her bra strap was showing.

"Jesus! Not only late but looking like that? Why did I bother getting out of bed this morning?" she thought. Setting her baggage on the sidewalk, she adjusted her clothing, then ran her fingers through the hair in a desperate attempt to make it stay put. Aware of the stares she was getting from people walking by, she shook her head in resignation. "Oh hell, I'm not going to get this contract anyway." She picked up her cases, set her shoulders straight and holding her head high, walked up to the reception desk.

"I have . . . had a ten-forty-five appointment with Mr. Diego," Marisha informed the girl behind the desk. The twenty-something cute receptionist asked her name, picked up the phone, punched some numbers, and then informed the person on the other end that the ten-forty-five had arrived. Hanging up, she pointed to the elevator.

"Fifth floor, they're waiting for you."

"Thank you."

In the elevator, Marisha made yet another attempt at getting herself presentable. She was extremely nervous. Three years ago, she'd be walking in there with confidence and determination not to fail. But this was now. She had two extra mouths to feed and, unlike three years ago, she needed every contract she could get her hands on. "Maybe if I come up with some whopper of an excuse, they'll forgive me for being late. Maybe if I beg? Dammit! I blew the chance of making some serious money."

Her high-heeled shoes clicked on the tiled floor of a hallway leading to another reception desk. A young woman greeted her with a friendly smile and a handshake.

"Hi, I'm Diana Finch. Oh please, let me help you with those." Diana came from behind the desk and took the biggest briefcase from Marisha. "Come with me," she smiled again.

"Thank you, and sorry I'm late . . ." Marisha started. Knocking on a glass door, Diana gently pushed it open. Marisha followed her inside. Diana poked her head into adjoining room. "Sir, Marisha Pawlak is here." Turning to Marisha she said, "Have a seat, please. He'll be right with you. Can I get you some coffee?"

Marisha shook her head, "No thank you." As much as she would love to have a cup, she didn't think she'd be here long enough to drink it.

"If you change your mind, I'll be at my desk," Diana said on her way out.

From the hushed, one-sided conversation next door, Marisha concluded that the man was on the phone. That gave her a couple of minutes to compose her thoughts. "I won't give him any excuses; I'll apologize for being late, and ask if he has time to look at some of my ideas. If he throws me out on my ear . . . screw him."

"Good morning." A male voice interrupted her thoughts.

Marisha turned her head towards the voice.

"Good mo . . . you! What?" The words died on her lips.

Hands in his pockets, Drake was casually leaning against the doorframe, smiling at her. Marisha's heart skipped a beat. He looked exactly the way she remembered, except for his hair. It was longer and without the gel holding it straight back, it looked softer. The same familiar jolt ripped through her body. It was as if no time had passed, as if she had just seen him yesterday. Her reaction frightened her.

"You're Mr. Diego?"

"Si, Drake Diego." He bowed and then came to stand beside her chair. Taking her hand, he lifted it to his lips. "It's good to see you," he whispered.

Marisha snatched her hand away. Scrambling to her feet, she looked for a way to get off the chair without bumping into him. Drake gently pushed her back.

"Don't run, it's okay, I just wanted to see you." He walked around the desk and slumped into a black leather chair.

She could have left. There was nothing standing between her and the door but Marisha didn't move. The four-foot wide mahogany desk provided enough distance between them and the panic she had felt earlier lessened considerably. Looking at Drake's sombre face, she couldn't stop herself from smiling. At home, she had two miniature replicas of him and she knew how easy it was to turn that frown into a heart-stopping smile.

"You're smiling, I like that." Drake said.

"It's so good to see you." Having a secret gave Marisha some confidence. "It's been a long time."

"Si." Drake put his elbows on the desk and folded his hands under his chin. A picture of this morning's breakfast scene came to mind and Marisha had to bite her lip to stop herself from laughing out loud. "This is too much," she thought. Surprised by her amusement, Drake's eyebrows met over the bridge of his nose, and his bottom lip came out far enough to give the impression of a pout. Marisha lost it. It was like looking at Josh through a magnifying glass. A tinny giggle escaped her lips.

"Why are you laughing at me?

"I'm sorry, you have me all mixed up. What are you doing here, Drake?"

"Taking care of business."

"Hmmm; a bartender from a Mexican tourist resort comes to Edmonton, to Nessex office building, to take care of business . . . uhmm . . . that makes perfect sense." Shaking her head, she turned serious. "Why are you here?" she repeated. Something set off a tiny little alarm inside her. "Does he know about Josh and Jenny? Is that the reason he came to Canada?" It was her turn to frown.

"You're not laughing anymore," Drake noted.

"Drake, you never give me a straight answer. It's always one or two words, not really telling me anything. Please, for once, answer my question fully. Why are you here?"

"I needed to see you. Also, I want you to decorate a hotel."

"I don't understand. Three years ago, when I met you, you were a bartender; today you're sitting here, talking about decorating a hotel . . . which hotel?" Marisha was going to get to the truth for once and for all. "Enough of this cat and mouse game, start talking," she demanded.

Drake leaned back in his chair. Biting his lower lip, he studied her face, looked down at her hands and then into her eyes.

"Why did you leave? You had another week."

"What difference does it make now? Drake, I'm warning you, either you tell me what the hell is going on, or I'm leaving right n . . ."

The ringing of the phone made them both jump. Drake picked it up.

"Hello?"

He listened for couple of minutes, spoke Spanish for a couple more, and other than "Adios" before he hung up, Marisha hadn't a clue as to what he was saying. Picking up the phone again, Drake issued an order. "Diana, bring us some coffee . . . and hold my calls."

Covering the mouthpiece, he asked Marisha, "Are you hungry?" She shook her head. "That's all, thank you." He replaced the receiver. Within seconds, Diana came in with a tray, placed it on the desk and quickly left the room.

Drake poured two mugs, brought one over to Marisha and set it on the desk. He reached for her hands and pulled her up. Standing face-to-face, holding hands and looking at each other brought back memories they had shared in Mexico. Drake lowered his head; Marisha reached for his kiss.

The feel of his lips, his scent and the warmth of his arms around her reminded her how much she had missed him. The strong feelings she felt for this man three years ago came back in an instant. He was the one who completed her, the other half of her heart.

With her arms around his neck, Marisha closed her eyes and let herself enjoy every second of his embrace. Nothing mattered right now, the contract, the twins—*the twins!*

Hands against his chest, she pushed him away. Reluctantly, Drake loosened his hold. The hurt look in his eyes didn't stop her from moving out of his reach.

"Marisha . . ." Drake started in a deep voice.

"No! Don't . . . I can't do this," she whispered.

"I know . . . I understand. We shouldn't have feelings for one another, but we do, we can't deny it. God knows I've tried . . . three years . . . three years . . . I can't get you out of my system. I know I'm going straight to hell . . . I know I'll pay for my sins, and still, I'm not able to walk away. It's like you've put a spell on me . . . I love you."

Drake made a step forward, but seeing Marisha step back, he walked behind the desk and fell into the leather chair, looking upset.

Marisha shifted her weight from one foot to the other. This was the most she'd ever heard him say. "But what is he telling me? What sins? Cheating on his wife . . . is that the reason he thinks he'll be punished? Did he say he loves me?"

"What are you saying, Drake? If you feel . . . er . . . felt like that, why did you walk away from me in Mexico? You left me in a driveway . . . you took off."

"You know why I left."

"No, I don't!"

"Don't play games with me. Secrets have a way of coming out, e-v-e-r-y time." He put stress on the last part.

"Drake, I have no idea what you're talking about. You're not making any sense. What secrets?" Marisha's patience was wearing thin.

"All the times you asked me if I'm married, what did you want to hear? That I had a wife, and like you, was just having a holiday fling? You demanded an answer. I avoided it. What was I supposed to do? If I told you I was married, you'd feel safe, but you'd hate me. And if I told you I wasn't married, you'd think that I wouldn't let you go . . . one way or the other, you'd run. I needed time with you, time to get to know you, and I didn't want to lie." Drake fell silent. Marisha was confused. She pulled her chair in front of the desk and leaning forward, looked directly at him.

"You have a way of dancing around the question without answering it. Did you ever think about telling me the truth?" she asked.

"Me? Tell you the truth? At least I didn't go around pretending to be single."

"Aha! So you are married! I knew it. You disgust me . . ."

Drake jumped to his feet, sending the office chair all the way to the back wall.

"So now I'm disgusting, am I? You didn't think so when you were making love to me in Mexico or a few minutes ago when you were kissing me. No, s-w-e-e-t-heart, don't you go all righteous on me, I'm not the one who is married!" Seeing the look of total surprise in Marisha's face, he placed his hands on the desk, leaned forward and looked directly into her eyes. "Si senora, I know!"

More confused than ever, Marisha had difficulty speaking.

"What . . . you . . . ?"

Drake had the floor now. Ignoring her attempt to speak, he continued.

"And the lengths you went to hide your status, Dios! Getting Max, Lilly and Ryan, even that Rhoda person, to collaborate with your lies! By the time I found out the truth, unfortunately, it was too late . . . by then I was in too deep. Blinded by feelings for you, my beliefs and my morals went out the window . . . and for what? You picked up and left anyway." He threw his hands in the air and turned his back on her.

Marisha sat silent, trying hard to make sense of his accusations. Her first thoughts were that he knew about the twins, but he kept going back to their time in Mexico. "Is he accusing me of running away from him . . . from Mexico . . . and does he think I'm married?"

"Drake, I'm not quite sure what I'm being accused of? What do you imagine I have lied to you about? You have no right to talk to me as if I've committed some sort of crime and you had to sacrifice your morals because of it. I don't know why I felt so drawn to you in Mexico but I was under the impression that you felt it too. Now you tell me that you did. So why? Why wouldn't you just tell me that you were single?" She watched him turn around.

"I've told you, I didn't want to lose you."

"You know, you're not making much sense, Drake."

"Think about it. Do I have to spell it out?"

"Please do," Marisha shot back.

Drake gave her a cross look, but pulled up the chair, sat down and drummed his fingers on the desktop before he spoke.

"For years, I have been avoiding any sort of commitment or relationship. Not telling a new acquaintance about my married or single status left me an option to use it later, to my advantage. I was doing the same when I first met you. Then I found out that you were married."

"Wait a cotton-picking minute! I'm not married."

"Don't deny it . . . your husband explained what you were doing."

"What husband? I don't have a husband!" Marisha jumped to her feet. "Me and Lilly, both single, working together, living in the same apartment block . . . doesn't that ring any bells?" she asked.

"Yeah, I remember. Max told me all that, but your husband said that you were all in it together."

"Together in what?"

"In helping you to have an affair."

"What?"

"Your husband said that you found out about his affair with your co-worker and he brought you to Mexico so you'd seduce someone and have your revenge. He told me that if I slept with you, I'd be doing both of you a favour and saving your marriage." Drake laughed unhappily. "Of course he was too late with his request; we'd already done the deed, several times. I wanted to walk then and there. I managed to stay away from you for one day and then I decided to take you away from the resort, get you to tell me the truth, hoping that maybe there was a remote chance I was wrong about your using me." Drake bit his lip and looked away from her. Marisha sat down again.

"Drake, the husband, did he tell you his name?"

"Greg, Greg Pawlak," Drake answered.

"Hmmm, so that's how he got rid of you." Unconsciously, Marisha's fingers went over the scar under her chin.

"Got rid of me? What are you talking about? I went away on business for half a day and when I got back, you were gone and so was your husband."

"Why didn't you ask Lilly where I was?"

Drake shrugged his shoulders. "What was the point? My guess was that you'd worked out your differences and went back home a happy couple," he said.

"So why are you here now?" she had to ask.

"I told you, I can't get you out of my mind. I needed to see you," he admitted shyly.

Seeing him so unhappy, Marisha's heart went out to him. She stood up and slowly walked over to his side. Pushing some papers out of the way, she sat down on top of the desk. He wasn't looking at her, so she reached out and placed her hand under his chin, gently turning his head to face her.

"Listen to me, Drake. Max was telling you the truth. I am not married and never have been. Greg was my first boyfriend, and I was going to marry him, but I didn't . . ."

She took her time explaining to Drake everything that had happened, about Greg's messing up her life, following her around, and Max's reason for being in Mexico. By the time she got to the reason why she had to leave the resort a week early, Drake was horrified by her story. Scooping her from the desk, he sat her on his lap and cradled her as one would a child. Marisha didn't resist.

CHAPTER 21

DIANA CHECKED HER watch. "I'm sorry sir, Mr. Diego is still in a meeting and he's not taking any calls." She listened for a moment, then started apologizing again. "I'm sorry, but I have my instructions . . . sir, please . . . sir . . . hello?" "Oh, how rude!" She tossed the phone on its cradle. Looking at her watch, she thought, "What are they doing in there? It's been over two hours! Shoot! I'm missing my lunch with Erica."

The list of phone messages was growing longer and her stomach was growling. Diana picked up the memo pad and walked towards the glass door. She knocked softly, but didn't get a response. She knocked again, still nothing. Turning the handle, she pushed the door open. Diego had the decorator on his lap and they looked as though they were about to kiss.

"Oh, gee, I'm so sorry . . . I . . ." she stuttered.

Drake cleared his throat. "Diana, what is it?" he snapped.

"Sorry . . . your messages, sir . . . and it's past lunch."

Drake cut her off. "Leave the messages on your desk and go to lunch," he ordered. Quickly and quietly, Diana made her retreat.

Marisha gave Drake a look. "That wasn't very nice," she said crossly.

"Her timing sucks. Anyway, you were telling me about Greg's arrest," he prompted.

"That's about it. He's in jail. I don't have to worry about being followed or spied on, end of my story. But you, you have some explaining to do Mr. Drake Diego."

"Now what? I've told you everything." Drake gave her a dazzling smile.

"Not so fast! I need to know how a bartender from Mexico ends up in Nessex office building, in Canada, looking for someone to decorate a hotel."

"Uh-oh, busted! I'm not really a bartender."

"Did you get fired?"

After a hearty laugh, Drake lifted her back to the desktop and retrieved their coffee mugs. "Rats, this is cold." He left the room to empty the cups into the sink. Returning, he refilled them and handed one to Marisha. "We should order lunch, I'm starving."

"Never mind food. What did you mean—you're not a bartender?"

"I'm not . . . well, I am . . . but I'm not."

"Drake!"

"Okay, okay, I've been in the resort business all my life. I can work any position including bartending. The time you came to Tropical

Palace, we were short of help and waiting for some workers to come from Cancun, so I was just filling in."

"That makes sense, but if you're not a full-time bartender, what is your job?"

Setting his cup down and clasping his hands behind his back, Drake rocked back and forth with laughter. "I own the Palace."

"You what?"

"I own the Palace, and several others," he said casually. "My family has been in the hotel business for decades."

"Why didn't you tell me that when we met?" Marisha asked.

"I didn't think it was important."

"But I felt bad for you. I thought that you got fired because of me."

"If I didn't own the joint, I would have been fired. The staff is not allowed to mingle with the guests . . . unless they are hired for entertaining," he explained.

"Drake, you're impossible."

"But you like me, si?"

Marisha slid off the desk and came to stand before him. "Si," she replied, wrapping her arms around his neck. "One more question. How come you're not married? A man with your looks, not to mention wealth, should be on his fifth or sixth divorce by now. Are you divorced?" she asked openly.

"No, I'm not divorced." Feeling Marisha stiffen up, he pulled her closer. "Never been married, no time for romance, never met the right person . . . until you came along. I guess I've been waiting for you all my life. Marisha, I love you. I've been in love with you from the moment I saw you. And for the past three years, I've spent hours looking at your pictures ..."

"My pictures? What pictures?" she asked, surprised.

"Tapes from the Palace's security cameras," he informed her. "Yeah, people started to look at me strangely!" Noticing Marisha's amusement, he shook her gently. "It's not funny, spending so much time in a dark little room, alone. Even I thought I was nuts. That's why I had to come and see you. Since I thought that you were married, I couldn't just show up at your doorstep. The perfect opportunity came up when we bought a hotel in Jasper. You work for a designer company; we need a decorator—it's a perfect excuse to see you."

"So that decorating job is for real?"

"Yours, if you want it."

"But you haven't even looked at my proposal." Marisha was very excited. She might land the contract after all. "What's the hell is wrong with me? It's Drake for God's sake! He came to see me and I'm thinking about a stinking contract." She took his face in her hands and pulled it to hers. "God, it's good to see you," she said, before their lips met.

Sometime later, Drake was buttoning his shirt. "Now I'm really, really hungry. Let's go and get something to eat," he begged.

Marisha smoothed her hair. "I really have to get back to the office ..."

"Marisha," he interrupted.

"Yes?"

"Marry me."

"Wh ... what?"

"Marry me ... please."

Marisha sucked in her breath. She stared at Drake, uncertain if he was toying with her or if he was serious. Drake paused, his hands still on the buttons, hair all messed up, and his bottom lip caught between his snow-white teeth. "Why are you looking at me like that?" he asked, all of a sudden nervous.

Marisha panicked. The reality of the situation hit her like a ton of bricks. He was serious! The man she'd fantasized about—the father of her children—had just asked her to marry him. With one simple word, her fantasies and daydreams could become a reality.

"Drake, before I can give you an answer, there is something I have to tell you."

"The only thing I want to hear is yes," he pressed.

"Yes, but a lot has happened since . . ."

"You said yes, you did say yes?" He took a step towards her.

"Wait . . ." Marisha waved her hand. She hadn't really meant "Yes" she'd marry him, she was simply acknowledging the fact that he wanted to hear her say it. Before she could do that, she had to tell him about the twins. "What if he doesn't want kids? Maybe he thinks it's too late to be tied up with family. What if he . . ."

Drake closed the short distance between them. Taking her in his arms, he said,

"I've waited long enough . . . no more waiting. You are free; I am free, why waste time? As it is, we've wasted too much of our lives just trying to find each other. We are meant to be together. You know it, and I know it." He pulled her body to his, and the passion they'd shared moments ago stirred up inside them again. "Too bad we didn't meet sooner; we could've given my parents a houseful of grandchildren," he said in a husky voice, pulling her blouse out of her skirt and running his hands over her naked back. Marisha couldn't resist. When it came to this man, she didn't posses an ounce of self-control. Her fingers went to work on the half-done buttons of his shirt.

Several minutes later, Marisha was tracing her finger over his lips. "Drake?"

"Si?" he answered lazily.

"Do you have any brothers or sisters?"

"Si, one brother."

"How old is he?"

"Same as me, forty-seven."

"That explains it," she thought. "I knew that the twins had to come from his side of the family." "Where is your brother?" she asked.

"Like me . . . wherever he's needed. Since our parents retired, we run the family business. Darcy and his wife, Theresa, look after the hotels and yours truly takes care of the resorts." Drake lifted himself on one elbow. "If you have any more questions you had better ask them quickly because I'm dying of starvation and I can't guarantee how much longer I'll live."

Marisha burst out laughing. She loved his sense of humour.

"Do Darcy and Theresa have children?"

"No. Momma prayed for grandchildren for over ten years, but her prayers went unanswered. Since I'm a lost cause, when Darcy and I are gone, there will be nobody to carry on the Diego family name. Papa is still holding out for me, but I think it's too late. I'll be fifty pretty soon. Now, I'm not answering another question without my lawyer present. It's cruel and unusual punishment to interrogate a man on an empty stomach." Drake got to his feet, and pulled Marisha up. "Get dressed, you vixen. We're going out."

Marisha's laughter died out, and serious again, she addressed him.

"Drake?"

One sleeve on, one off, Drake stopped dressing and looked at her in dismay. "No, no, no, have you no mercy, woman?"

"This can't wait . . . I need to tell you something," she said awkwardly, not having the courage to look at him. Seeing her face so serious, Drake came to her and lifted her chin with one finger. "What's wrong my love? Why so gloomy?" he asked softly.

"Your mom, she . . . she doesn't know it yet, but her prayers were answered. She has a grandchild, well, two grandchildren." Searching his face for reaction to this news, Marisha added, "You have two children."

Drake took a step back. "What are you talking about? That's not funny!"

"I'm telling you that you have two children . . . I came home from Mexico pregnant."

"You're serious . . ." He raked his hair with his hands. "Two?"

"Twins . . . a boy and a girl."

Turning his back to Marisha, he slowly walked to sit behind his desk. The black eyebrows touching, lower lip totally covered by the upper one, Drake sat frozen.

"Say something," Marisha begged.

"How old?"

His voice was so low that Marisha wasn't sure what he'd said. "What?" she asked.

"How old are they?" he asked quietly.

"Two years old." She made a move towards him. "Drake . . ."

"Stay there." His voice held a warning. "Tell me their names."

Marisha froze. She didn't expect him to be angry. From what he'd told her about his family, she was sure that after the initial shock, he'd be happy with her news. Obviously, she was wrong. Drake looked as though he could murder her with his bare hands.

"Their names are Josh and Jenny," she said.

Soundlessly, his lips formed the names several times. Then he stood up, and pierced her with his eyes.

"Two years old! And you didn't think it necessary to let me know that I have a son and a daughter? What if I hadn't come looking for you? Would you ever have let me know? Dios! How could you keep something like that from me? I'm a father . . ." He fell heavily into the chair. "I'm a father. I have children," he was saying to himself.

"Drake, please, let me explain." Tears of disappointment blurred her vision. Seeing Drake's reaction, she knew now that keeping the children from him was by far the worst thing she'd ever done. Disappointed in herself and ashamed of her selfishness, despite his earlier warning, Marisha came to stand beside Drake's chair.

"There are no words to describe how sorry I am for keeping the babies a secret. When I came back from Mexico and found out that I was pregnant, nothing would've made me happier than sharing the joy with you. But you were not here. I didn't hear from you. Lilly said you never even asked about me. What was I supposed to do? I couldn't go looking for you . . . if you were married, and I was almost certain that you were, I didn't want to cause problems. The pregnancy wasn't easy, and between my job and the doctors, I was too preoccupied to think how unfair I was being to you. Please, try to understand my position. Don't hate me," she pleaded.

Drake wasn't looking at her. His jaw was set, and his eyes were fixed on the far wall. After what seemed like an eternity of silence, she heard him say, "I don't hate you."

Slowly, he roused himself and stood facing her. "I don't hate you," he repeated.

Marisha reached for him, and he took her in his arms. There were no sparks, no passion, just an embrace of comfort for both.

"You can forget that decorating contract," he whispered into her ear.

She pushed at his chest. "You said that you didn't hate me."

"I don't . . . I love you. But because of that criminal, Greg, I was denied you . . . and my children. We're getting married immediately and we're taking our children somewhere warm and quiet, so we can get to know each other. We can't do that if you're working. I'm going to take few months off, and so will you. We owe it to ourselves and our children . . . our children." Drake's voice broke. Then, the smile on his face lit up the sparks in his eyes. "Our children! I love that sound," he said.

Marisha's heart was singing with joy. Drake loved her and loved the idea of being a daddy. She locked her fingers behind his neck.

"About the wedding," she started.

"Don't even think about arguing."

"Who's arguing? All I wanted to ask was if we could get married at the Tropical Palace in Mexico, that's all."

"Wherever you wish, as long as we don't have to wait. Now, take me home to my children, woman." He tried to sound tough, but the beginning of a grin gave him away.

"I thought that you were hungry. Don't you want to go and eat?" she teased.

"Oh boy, I can see that I'll have my hands full with you."

"And you'll love it." She kissed his nose. "Si?"

"Si." Drake kissed her back.

THE END

CPSIA information can be obtained at www.ICGtesting.com
Printed in the USA
LVOW122102030112

262228LV00001B/3/P